The Last Woman

JACQUELINE DRUGA

VULPINE
PRESS

The Last Woman by Jacqueline Druga
Copyright © 2018 Jacqueline Druga

Originally self-published by Jacqueline Druga in 2014
Published by Vulpine Press in the United Kingdom 2018

ISBN: 978-1-910780-50-3

Cover by Claire Wood

www.vulpine-press.com

ACKNOWLEDGMENTS

Thank you, Sophia and Sami, for all your help on this one.

This book is dedicated to Fred M. After all of your support, I don't believe I have ever dedicated a book to you. So, this one is for you. Thanks so much for your unending support.

1. WAKING

At first there was nothing.

Nothing kicked in. Void of all my senses, I was stuck in a momentary state of confusion. Was it Saturday, or did I have to work? The alarm clock didn't go off—or did it? I lingered in that plane of existence between awake and asleep, that fine-line moment just after a deep sleep and a bizarre dream. But I didn't dream. My faculties escaped me.

That was only briefly.

The moment I came to, I opened my eyes and immediately panicked.

What happened? Where was I?

My thought processes kicked in along with my senses.

Sight.

Everything was black. I couldn't see an inch in front of my face. I shifted my eyes—nothing but darkness.

What was going on? *Think, Faye, think.*

I tensed up, forcing my memory. Why couldn't I remember?

My legs were heavy, as if weighted down. Something was on them. My left arm wouldn't budge; my right hand tingled. With every blink, I felt something brush against my eyelashes.

Think.

A bit of a memory—a flash, more like it.

Christine. She was laughing. Her face distorted in my mind as if seen through blurry goggles.

She tossed back her blonde hair. "You have to be joking," she said.

My laugh. I heard myself laugh.

Girls' night out. That was it. The last thing I remembered.

"Are you kidding me?" Amber reached out, covering my glass. "She doesn't need any more. She's drunk enough. You've had enough, Faye."

"She's a big girl," Christine said. "Besides, let her drink. She needs to forget the pain."

The pain. That's right—my heartache. But somehow I couldn't grasp that, because my head pounded like nothing I'd ever felt.

The darkness, the blackout. Immediately I wondered if I'd fallen victim somehow.

Get it together. Get it together.

I blinked again—it was so hard to breathe—and then I realized something was covering my face. Some sort of coarse cloth. Turning my head side to side, I could feel it graze against my cheeks. It covered my nostrils; just tilting my head made it easier to take in air.

Wherever I was, whatever had happened, I was trapped. But not completely. I moved my right hand.

I opened my mouth to call for help, but my tongue stuck to the roof of my mouth, pasted there, swollen. Moving my lips immediately caused them to crack painfully. I felt the tension of my skin and the tear, then the warm blood as it rolled across my lips.

It made its way into my mouth, and as gross as it was, as metallic as it tasted, it was moisture. I absorbed it.

A knot formed in my stomach, like a baseball turning and hurting with each twist. I raised my right arm and pushed on the fabric. It had a give to it.

If I could move, I could get out. That was my thought process as I assessed my situation.

My legs were pinned. I was indeed naked. For sure, someone had abducted me. I'd blacked out from so much drinking, and that was what happened. How long was I out? Long enough to be pained with thirst and sick with hunger, and for my legs to be glued together by a thin moisture I could only assume was my own bodily functions.

I turned my head, arching my neck. "Help!" I cried, hoarse and emotional.

No one replied.

Was there even a sound? Yes, there was. A buzzing, a continuous, deep buzzing. Then another sense kicked in.

Smell. That knot of hunger in my gut turned to nausea at the rotten, sulfurous smell of bad food. A stench that I should have noticed right away, but I'd been too consumed with everything else.

What was it? Garbage. That was it. I'd been dumped in the garbage.

If anything, I was not a quitter.

It was fear that caused an instinctive physical fight, right there and then. Scared out of my wits, I push the fabric with my right arm while struggling with my legs.

I diligently forced my left hand down and it sunk into a soft, squishy surface. I had to get a grip, not just emotionally, but physically.

Rock back and forth, use my hips, repetitive motions. *Think, think, think …*

"Where is everyone?" I asked. "It's dead in here tonight."

"News is saying stay inside."

"Oh my God, please. It's the flu."

"I got my shot."

Laughter.

4

"I had a drink."

Rock again. Back and forth, back and forth, almost there.

"Faye, you okay?"

"Hey, she doesn't look okay."

Left arm free, right leg ... Kick.

"She's not okay. Faye!"

"Someone call 911!"

Free!

Released from whatever had confined me, I felt the air against my nude body as I rolled away. Freedom from that prison ejected me in a downward tumble, shoulder over shoulder, banging, bouncing against the steep, soft mound, until I landed.

I had twisted within the cloth wrapped around my head, and not only did it cover my face, but it was tangled around my neck, choking me.

I coughed and wheezed, fighting to free myself. I pulled at the cloth in a panic as I felt something stinging my legs. Tiny dots of burning danced about my body and the buzzing grew louder.

No!

I yanked as hard as I could, scratching my neck with my finger-nails as I whipped the heavy cloth from my head. The sun was so bright I had to close my eyes. I was blinded. Cloth still in my hand, I brought it to my face as a shield and slowly opened my eyes.

The pain in my legs grew worse. What was biting me?

Finally, through the blur of the sun, I was able to cast enough shadow over my eyes to see, and I looked down.

Flies. Thousands of flies covered my legs.

I kicked and squirmed and rolled over to my knees. The second I tried to stand up, my legs weakened, buckled, and I fell back down. I grabbed the mound to gain balance.

After a moment, my eyes started to adjust. Head down, I was filled with horror when I saw my fingers had gripped a body.

I screamed and quickly withdrew my hands. I was on my knees. I slowly lifted my head.

The final sense kicked in.

Realization.

I hadn't been abducted and dumped in the garbage. I was a number. Four thousand seven hundred and twenty-three. A tag hung from my wrist, stating such.

Someone had made a mistake.

I couldn't move or breathe. I could only look around. I was in a football stadium. Somewhere near the end zone. The field goal was just to my left, but the bottom portion was buried like everything else. Buried beneath a never-ending mound. A mound as high and as far as I could see of nothing but dead bodies.

2. STANDING

It was a nightmare. It had to be.

To go from being out with friends who were trying to take my mind off things to ending up in a football stadium maxed out with bodies was nothing less than a nightmare.

I was dreaming.

Wake up.

I tried to find a spot on the field where my feet didn't touch rotting flesh. The soft surface of decaying bodies wasn't firm enough to support my already weakened legs.

My God, wake up!

I tried to stand and my legs cramped, sending me buckling back to the mound.

My knees sank into a mushy pile. I looked down. It was greenish, red and black, a sticky tar-like substance, strands of which followed my knees when I stood again. Even with my eyesight not at a hundred percent, I could see the maggots squirming in the flesh.

A knotted and empty stomach produced no vomit. My body reacted as if it would. Retching, heaving. Releasing dry spasms.

Get it together. Wake up!

The longer I fought to stand, the more the sights and smells took over and the more I realized I was already awake.

"Hello!" I cried out. "Someone!"

There were so many bodies that my voice didn't even carry an echo in the stadium. It did, however, stir the flies, which swarmed my way.

I didn't have the strength to stand there. I had to get out. Someone had made a mistake. They'd dumped me with all these bodies.

And where did the bodies come from? That was the only thing that truly made me believe I was in some sort of lucid dream. If I was four thousand something or other, how many were there? It was impossible. The pile of corpses was so big, the only way it would reach that height was if the bodies were air dumped.

That many, though?

Life was normal, at my last recollection. A week earlier there had been a country concert right where I now stood.

Had war broken out? Maybe a chemical or biological attack? That would explain it.

That was it. That had to be it. Mass casualties of war.

I saw a tag on a nearby body and reached out. The hand had perfectly manicured nails. There was an "F" on the tag—female. The number was thousands higher than mine.

Seeing that left me breathless.

How did I not die? Not get crushed? For a few minutes, I was pummeled by thoughts and questions.

Whatever the cause—and I could guess all I wanted—I knew I had to get out of there. I had been abandoned as a casualty. My body was in dire need of water and possibly medical attention. I didn't know.

But one thing I was certain of—I was alone. No one was there to help me. At least, not in the stadium—outside, maybe in the corridors, yes. But in that massive grave, I was just a number.

I lifted the cloth I'd been shrouded in and did a half-assed job of wrapping it around my shoulders. It covered some, better than nothing. With my legs aching and weak, I took the first of many small, unstable steps, determined to get off that field.

3. EMERGENCE

The heat of the sun helped warm up my body. There were two ways out of the stadium—walk to the tunnel that led to the locker room or venture up the steps. I wasn't familiar with the place, having only been there once. Something told me, though, that taking the tunnel would be a challenge; it would be dark and cold. At least, I believed so. Even though the stairs stretched way ahead of me, they would get me out of the stadium easier.

My legs held up as I tackled the steps, focusing forward and not looking back at what was behind me.

I was so thirsty my mouth and throat burned. They felt swollen. There was no way I'd been forgotten about for more than a few days. No way I could have survived that long without water. Step by step, I forged ahead, hoping I wouldn't fall, wishing I had been closer to the scoreboard, because that would have been an easier route.

In my mind I was envisioning some sort of military set up, or at least the body garbage men, when I reached the concession level. Looks of utter shock and surprise when they saw me. Someone calling out, "Dear God, where did you come from?"

Then water; they'd give me water to drink, and swiftly take me to get cleaned and dressed.

I was pretty certain the only medical attention I needed was nourishment. Nothing felt broken. Then again, my body was still numb with shock.

No sooner had I reached the first level of the stadium than I realized my thoughts of rescue were mere fantasies. There wasn't a soul around. My bare feet echoed against the cool concrete. I readied to call out, but stopped.

What was I thinking?

I really wasn't thinking about much except how to get out. Immediately, I felt riddled with fear and anxiety. I was scared to death that someone was going to shoot me, or jump out. There was a reason all the bodies had accumulated that quickly; and for some stupid reason, the bodies had been an afterthought, as if by leaving the stadium I was leaving the reality that thousands of people had died somehow.

With death comes insanity.

With that much death, people wouldn't be in their right mind.

What was the event that I'd missed?

All that would come; I'd find my answers after I safely found my way out of the death stadium and got help.

Inching cautiously forward, I stopped to peek every few feet. Look and listen. The only light seemed to come from the sun, which was making its way in through the open level. But it was dark, shadowed and cold.

I stayed close to the wall, as if it afforded me protection.

The corridors were wide and hollow, the concession stands closed up. But it was quiet—my God, was it quiet. There had to be people outside. A body receiving setup, or something. Surely they didn't come inside, not with the smell and the flies.

I was rank, nauseated by my own odor. I smelled of the dead and my own excretion. Glancing at my hands, I saw bruising just below the knuckles, dried blood. At some point there had obviously been an IV in my hand. One someone just ripped out.

Using the light as my guide, hoping it was the exit, I noticed the side door to one of the concession places was ajar.

Please. Please let there be something there to drink. Even though I knew salvation and help weren't that far away, I needed water. The desire was all too consuming, so much so that I could barely think of anything else.

I peered through the crack of the slightly open door; no one was there and I went in.

There was an inviting case of water in a cabinet. I slid open the door and grabbed a bottle. One would have thought the cap was glued on, it was so hard to open. It was warm, but I guzzled it. I knocked back the entire twenty ounces, finding recovery in each sweeping wave of liquid that passed into my mouth. I felt it bulge in my throat, pour down my esophagus and straight into my empty stomach.

Mistake.

No sooner had I finished the bottle than my stomach knotted. The water erupted out of my mouth faster than I had consumed it.

I felt foolish, as if someone were watching me. Taking a moment, I let my stomach settle before grabbing another bottle. Out of the corner of my eye, I spotted the chip rack. Just in case, just on the off chance no one was outside, I grabbed a bag and a third bottle of water. I held them tightly and forged into my second attempt at hydration.

This time, I sipped. Brought it into my mouth, swished it around and slowly allowed it to pass down my throat.

Third sip in, I heard the first sound that wasn't a buzzing insect.

It was a short creak, then a bang. Sounded like metal. It repeated. Creak. Bang. Creak. Bang. Immediately, I was overwhelmed with excitement. Someone was there. And then, in a flip-flop of emotions, I panicked.

Metal. What if someone was locking the gate to the death trap? Locking it, securing it and possibly destroying it.

With renewed vigor brought on by my need for help, I hobbled as fast as I could toward the sound.

"Wait! Don't go!" I cried out. "Wait! I need help. Help!" The entire way there, I called. "Wait! Stop! Help!"

Turning the bend, the anxiety and excitement dropped away.

Again, no one.

The sound continued. It was the gate to the stadium. Open, it swung slightly in the wind. Opening, closing. Creak. Bang.

On the verge of defeat, I caught a glimpse of a brown tent just outside. A military tent. Near it, a truck. I sighed in relief. Help was just outside. I pushed forward, opened the gate, stepped outside.

I froze.

There wasn't a soul around. The only sound was the flapping of the tent in the breeze. It had been set up by the water fountain that had just been erected the summer before. The fountain wasn't running; it was merely a shallow pool of water. The door to the huge military truck was open, but I couldn't see any soldiers.

"Hello!" I screamed, as loud as I could.

Hollow.

Desolate.

My voice echoed back at me.

I turned clockwise, looking for any signs of people, but there were none.

A huge emptiness consumed me. I felt overwhelmed by the ambience of ... nothing.

Where was everyone?

4. HOLDING POST

I lost it.

Immediately I broke. Any smidgeon of bravery I'd had within me vanished and I crumbled. I dropped to the ground and sobbed. The sounds of my own sadness echoing back at me magnified my emotions.

How long did I kneel there crying? I don't know. I didn't have enough liquid in me to produce actual tears, but the emotion was the same. My body shuddered with sadness.

I was there long enough that my legs tensed and cramped up. Long enough dwelling in my own self-pity and fear that I eventually came full circle and convinced myself to snap out of it and get it together.

It was one part of the city. A single part of one city. I just needed to venture further.

A barricade of roadblock horses was set up just beyond the concrete walkway to the stadium. Beyond that there was a truck, and it was clearly filled with bodies. But there was only one tent.

It certainly wasn't a medical setup, not with one tent.

I made my way over to it, preparing for the worst. I caught the aroma as soon as I got close. Death. I smelled death. Leaving my water and chips at the empty table just outside the tent, I held my nose and lifted the flap.

It was a field office, or perhaps a temporary home. Besides a desk, there were four cots, two of which held bodies. Both were men, still in uniform, partially covered. Their weapons were at the feet of their cots along with duffle bags. As if they had come to stay for a while but never made it out of bed. Their faces were swollen, blackened and splotched. There was dried blood around their noses. I wasn't an expert, so it was hard for me to tell if those were the effects of decomposition or effects of what had killed them.

I don't know why, but I felt really bad. Whatever had taken their lives did so while they diligently held their posts. Holding their jobs, serving their country until the very last second.

I took a moment, then walked to each of them and lifted the covers over their heads. It was something respectful I could do for them. At least they weren't part of a huge mound of bodies. Dumped there and forgotten. They weren't, to me, a number, a nameless person. In fact, they both still wore their military jackets, names clear on their chests.

Stevens. Wilkes.

As I turned, I saw the desk more clearly. There was a radio on top and a clipboard with a two-inch-thick stack of papers.

Answers.

Or so I thought.

A man's wristwatch sat on top of the clipboard, just above the writing on the plain white paper.

Unable to continue. Please give this to my mom. Wilkes. May 3.

May third?

I lifted the sheet to see what was written next. Figures and charts, things I couldn't make heads or tails of, except one thing.

Filled to capacity—May 1. Awaiting cleansing orders.

Apparently, Wilkes and Stevens had been awaiting orders that never came.

I lifted the wristwatch, an older model, wind up. It showed evidence of wear and tear, discoloration from the years. As my fingers grazed over it, I felt engraving on the back. It said "Happy Anniversary," with a date from over twenty years earlier. Maybe it had belonged to Wilkes' father. I turned the watch over and my eyes went directly to the date display. May fifth. At the most they had been dead for two days.

No sounds emerged from the radio. I lifted it from the base, played with the knobs on top until I heard a hiss of static.

I depressed the side button. "Hello?"

Static.

"Anyone there?"

Hiss.

How many times did I turn the channel button, calling out, with no response?

Oh my God. What was happening?

It was May fifth.

Wait. I pressed my memory. The accident was on February first, a date painfully embedded in my soul. The trial ... April second. What day did Christine and Amber take me out? I had been a recluse for weeks, drinking myself into oblivion. Consuming so much alcohol on a daily basis, I don't think I knew what sober was anymore.

Tax day. April fifteenth.

My God, I'd lost three weeks. And not only was I wondering how I'd lost three weeks, I was wondering how that many people had died that quickly.

It had to be war, as I'd thought previously. And unfortunately, I was in a section of the city that had been evacuated.

Only the dead remained.

I left the tent, grabbing my half-finished bottle of water and sipping it as I walked.

What if I just needed to step out more, look further than the confines of the stadium grounds—maybe I would see something. A sign, perhaps. Surely if they'd evacuated there would be signs.

The stadium was close to the river, and I could feel the breeze coming from it. There was a stench, too.

Walk toward the river, look for the bridges. Quarantines, movement, something would be on one of the bridges.

Find a direction.

I didn't make it far. Only far enough to see the river, and then I knew—whatever had happened was bigger than a section of the city. Bigger than just a stadium filled with bodies.

There were thousands of corpses, an endless flow drifting downstream.

5. WATCHING AND LEARNING

I sat on the steps of the amphitheater, sipping my water and eating creamed chicken from an MRE—a Meal, Ready to Eat ration pack—as I watched the bodies float down the river.

It was surreal, like a dream that wasn't really happening.

The bodies didn't stop. Once in a while they thinned out, a single body here and there rather than groups, but they kept coming. Where from?

Leaving the city and getting out of the death was foremost on my mind. Somehow, I had been left there in a place that was completely dead. Not a sound. No birds, no dogs, nothing.

I knew that it had been at least days since I'd had some sort of nourishment pumped into me via IV, and if I was going to get out I needed to regain some strength. That began with rehydration.

My headache started to subside. I attributed that to the water.

Before taking my seat on the steps, I had returned to the tent. There were answers there; I just had to decipher them.

I remembered the duffle bag, and I went to retrieve that along with the clipboard, radio and watch.

Opening the bag was like discovering a gold mine. There were pants, a T-shirt, socks and a shaving kit. Wilkes had the smaller boots, and I took them.

Before getting into the clothes, I took his bar of soap and stepped into the fountain. The water was cold and sort of clean. It took my breath away, but I got used to it and eventually submerged myself. I knew the water was old, but compared to what had collected on my body, it didn't matter.

I honestly felt like my skin absorbed that fountain water; it refreshed me much like a shower used to after a hangover.

I got dressed; the clothes were too big for me, but it was better than being naked. It was on my initial examination of the truck that I spotted the MREs and blankets. There weren't many ration packs, and I learned from a simple glance at the clipboard that early on, people had gone there for food. It was a distribution and drop-off center.

I took a blanket; the remaining MREs I'd save for when I left the city. But for the moment, I needed to get enough strength up to leave the immediate area.

Blanket draped over me, eating my food, I watched the bodies. Everything that had transpired, everything that had brought me to that particular moment on the steps of the amphitheater, was a mystery I needed to unravel.

The clipboard was a start. The last page bore the earliest date—signed by Stevens, an arrival report dated April 20.

I truly believed that once I'd regained my strength, my memory of the missing days would come back to me. At least, bits and pieces.

I stayed on the steps until the sun started to set, just before seven. I made sure to wind the watch; I didn't want that to die.

It was going to be dark soon, and there didn't seem to be power anywhere. It would be too dark to travel.

Though a little more hydrated and no longer hungry, I still felt weak.

I made my way back to the abandoned military supply truck, climbed in the front, shut the doors and locked them.

I'd rest there for the evening and read from the clipboard until I was finished or fell asleep, learning all that I could. After all, what else was there to do?

Then in the morning, I'd gather only what I needed and could carry, and I'd find my way out. I may have been alone in that part of the city, but there was no way, no how, that I was completely alone.

I was alive; others had to be as well. No matter how many bodies were piled up in the stadium or floating down the river, it wasn't conceivable that I was the only one who remained. I was convinced of that. Convinced there would be help and others out there; I just needed to get out of this area and across the river to find them.

6. SLIGHT REMEMBRANCE

I'd be lying if I said my own thoughts didn't scare me. I was creating things that weren't there, noises that didn't exist and shadows that were impossible.

Locked in the cab of the truck, I lost count of how many times I turned the interior light on and off. It was society putting the crazy thoughts in my head. Movies, to be exact. Not that I was a fan, but I had seen them, laughed them off and dismissed them. But truth be known, a part of me did fear seeing a staggering, recently risen person out for my blood. Or even someone crazed and virus-infected, racing madly toward me with no regard for their own pain.

Although if the dead were rising, I would have been corned beef hash, waking up among thousands of bodies.

I tried to get some sleep, but that wasn't happening. I wasn't feeling well at all. My legs were weak, my stomach cramped, and I swam in nausea. It had to be from eating. My system wasn't processing it. I hadn't a clue when they had dumped me in the pile.

I was still trying to figure out how that had happened. Apparently, from the mark on my hand and also the interior fold of my elbow, I had been receiving medical attention.

What turned? What made them think I was dead? Maybe they didn't know, didn't check or even care. I was one less person to care for and deal with. Get rid of me, toss me, I wasn't going to survive. No one would know anyhow.

Sitting there in the truck, juggling between trying to sleep, jumping in fear and reading the soldiers' notes, I started to recall that night. That last night with Christine and Amber.

I wasn't on a downer; I was in my new state, comfortably numb, lacking emotions and not really caring if I lived or died. How ironic, considering I'd been struggling to survive since I rolled from the heap of bodies. Wanting to live. How long I'd be that way remained to be seen.

That night though, I was already drinking when they arrived. I wasn't drunk, not by a long shot. My steady diet of bourbon made me feel invincible to the stuff, almost as if I'd built up an intolerance to getting good and drunk.

Christine made me laugh. She always did. Perhaps that was why I'd avoided talking to her over the phone or seeing her since the accident. Amber was solid and motherly; she fed into my depression. Not Christine, she didn't even need to try and she'd make me laugh.

She was that person who lit up a room just by walking in. Her sarcastic humor, witty one-liners. She was a natural—and I just didn't want any part of smiling.

We hit the hibachi place. I barely ate, but I did about four shots of sake and then we went to our favorite hangout. There were a lot of younger people, and we enjoyed their energy and antics.

But on that night, the typical Saturday night "having a blast" crowd was thin. There were tables, lots of empty tables.

"Where is everyone?" I asked. "It's dead in here tonight."

"News is saying stay inside," Amber said.

"Oh my God, please. It's the flu," Christine said bluntly. "The flu. This happens like every five years—they act like this is the big one. Remember SARS?"

"MERS, too," Amber said.

"And don't forget The Great Return of the Swine Flu." Christine poured me a drink from the pitcher.

"I got my shot," Amber said, "but that was in November."

Christine laughed at that for some reason. A forty-year-old woman shooting alcohol from her nostrils in a snort of laughter. "It's not even cold and flu season."

The flu.

I know I didn't have it, not that night. What had happened to me simply had to be alcohol poisoning. I overdid it. The room started to spin, my hands went numb, and despite what I thought I was saying, what came from my mouth was only a jumbled mess.

But it wasn't the flu. Not then, anyhow.

Other bits and pieces of memory came back. Coming to here and there, never for long.

"She's showing signs of the flu."

"How can she have the flu, she's been in the hospital." Then whoever said that coughed.

"And you need to ask?"

Cough.

But what difference did it make if I'd had the flu?

Was that even possible? That something like that could bring a city to its knees? The last I'd heard, we hadn't even had a case of the new virus in America.

The rational person in me couldn't fathom that some flu had caused thousands of bodies to float down a river. It was the same rational side that insisted the dead weren't rising and I was out of my mind for thinking about it.

No, it was something else. I had all those reports and notes from Wilkes; I just had to read through them and make heads or tails out of them.

I wouldn't believe it until I had to. What had occurred in my city, in my mind, was a single event. It had to be, because the prospect of anything greater than that was too frightening for me to even think about facing.

7. COMPANY OF STRANGERS

It was the longest night of my life. Perhaps because I went into the truck before the sun had set, afraid to leave and venturing out only to use the portajohn.

I didn't hear any crickets or cicadas, only the buzz of flies. They didn't sleep. And as the night grew darker, the moon hidden by the clouds, the flies swarmed to the light from the truck, covering the windshield. I'd smack my hand against it; they'd buzz away, but would return shortly after.

It became tiresome, trying to read the reports when the first one was at the bottom of the stack. I spent some time shuffling the papers, putting them in chronological order from top to bottom. The only thing that remained in the same spot was the note that Wilkes had written about getting his watch to his mother.

I left that on top. To me, that was heartbreaking, knowing that the young man, even in his illness, at the end of his life, was thinking about his mother.

How would his mother feel, knowing her child was sick and there was nothing she could do? As a mother myself, I took some sort of comfort in the fact that my own son and daughter, my own husband, didn't have to face the horrors of whatever had wiped out our city.

His name was Jason Wilkes, and he and countless others kept me company in the truck all night.

Jason, whether he was in charge or not, signed each and every report. SSG Jason A. Wilkes. Whatever the "SSG" meant, I didn't know and it didn't matter. To me he was Jason Wilkes.

His wallet was in his duffle bag. He was thirty-one years old, brown hair, blue eyes, lived in North Carolina. His license was expiring in a month, and from a picture I found it looked like he had a daughter. One government-issued credit card and three dollar bills. Otherwise, the wallet was jam-packed with useless receipts.

Well, not useless. They told me about him. Where he ate, what he bought, where he was. I looked at each one of them, trying to understand the man who thought about his mother when he was at death's door. The man who took time every day, several times a day, to fill out reports and make notations. The young man who had such a hard job.

He not only noted rations, but he and the other soldier, Stevens, were the men of the dead.

There was more at the desk than just reports. Off to the side, stacked up, were boxes of blank tags, like the one on my wrist.

Jason had probably filled it out.

More than that, there were boxes of wallets and billfolds, identification cards secured with rubber bands. All items retrieved from the deceased as they were banished from their names and given a number.

Because none of the credit cards or cash in the wallets had been touched, I assumed Jason Wilkes was ambitious. Perhaps he had intended to use the identification cards and licenses to write down and record all the names of the dead. Or maybe even notify families. Whatever the reasons, the boxes were there, and I grabbed one to rummage through.

I leafed through each wallet, each license, taking my time with them. It wasn't just something to do—it was my homage. It was what needed to be done.

I'd lift a license, look at the picture. "Theresa Lange. I'm sorry for what happened to you."

Next.

"William Jameson. I'm sorry for what you went through."

Every license in the box.

Every piece of identification represented a body that was part of a huge mound inside the stadium. But unlike me, they hadn't sat up and said, "I'm alive."

Their light of existence was over, snuffed out and reduced to the desecration of a mass grave of countless dead.

Was that who they were? Did they deserve that?

No.

For their families, for them, and their suffering, even if it was only me doing it, for one moment they weren't a casualty. They were more than a body in a pile, more than a number. They were a person with a face, a life, and they were being acknowledged and remembered.

8. THE FOCUS

I jolted awake from a dream that immediately escaped me. I peered down at the Wilkes watch. It was only 9:00 a.m. My mouth was dry and my head hurt, and those were the least of my physical worries.

I felt bad. Weak.

My legs were rubbery and my stomach kept flopping. In my condition, I didn't see myself walking out of the city or making any great distance. Not until I got my strength back.

Returning to the military camp was always an option, but going on the assumption that I wouldn't, I took the supplies I needed and the clipboard and placed them in Wilkes' duffle bag.

It was heavy, and I suppose I could have left behind some water bottles, but I didn't know what had happened to the city. Had people wiped out stores in a panic binge for survival supplies? I knew what the city was like before a snowstorm, and I didn't want to take any chances.

I also took something else—the keys to the supply truck. While I couldn't see myself driving it, I needed it to be an option.

There was a bright side to the morning. Only a few bodies floated down the river. Was it the last of them, or were they just done dumping them?

The dark side was the bridges. Of the two I could see, one was completely barricaded, the other destroyed.

To get out the city, eventually I would have to cross a bridge. They had to have been closed on April 26. Wilkes had written that they'd arrived on the twentieth, and noted that they dealt with panic on the twenty-sixth, when lockdown went into effect.

Lockdown. Quarantine.

I learned a lot about the first few days.

Beatrice Wilson was the first body to arrive at the stadium grave. At least, I assumed that. Wilkes had etched her name with the hashtag symbol and the number one on the report stating the arrival of the first bodies. He was trying to keep track. He really was.

The stadium was located in what had originally been a depressed area, converted into a riverside cultural section. If people were alive, if there were signs or newspapers, surely I'd find them if I wandered out.

My plan was to stay close to the stadium, making it my retreat point if I fell ill again.

I needed a focus, a goal; wandering aimlessly wouldn't do me any good. I wasn't out looking for food, but I didn't rule out shoes or clothes. I needed those.

Focus one—I wanted to find out more about what had happened. From what I'd gathered from the reports, some sort of event had caused people to die in masses. Actually, in waves; numbers on the reports, as well as the number of reports, increased with each day.

However, nothing Wilkes had written said what that event was. Why would it—they were current status reports. Or rather, they described distribution and graves.

Focus two—people. While I didn't need them, I wanted to find people. I was alone; I didn't want to be alone, nor did I want to move out of the city by myself. On a survival scale of one to ten, I probably ranked a two. My biggest venture into survival had been when the power went out for two days and I didn't have air-conditioning. My answer to that was a hotel.

And maybe a hotel was the answer to finding people.

Where would they go? Aside from hospitals and their own homes, where would they go?

If they were trapped in the quarantine zone, they were either looking for a way out or a way to survive. They'd search for food and water, go someplace where there would be supplies. Stores, gas stations, hotels, restaurants, bars. There were a lot of bars in the area.

Final focus—a way to get out of the blocked city. It didn't matter how—I didn't just want to get out of the city, I wanted to get home.

My home.

9. VENTURING OUT

There was a pair of binoculars in the back of the supply truck, and I deemed them my most valuable find of the morning. The city was nestled on three rivers that formed a "Y". It relied heavily on bridges to bring commuters into the downtown area. On the edge of the river, I used the binoculars to check out the bridges. The one to the west was destroyed, as were those south of the city itself. But one bridge, the one not far from me that only went into the downtown area, was only barricaded. It made me wonder whether the event had only taken place in town and toward the north side. The place where I stood and where the bodies were dumped.

I tried to see the city, and it wasn't easy. What I could make out was still a long way away, and I didn't notice any movement at all. That didn't mean there were no people there. That was my goal for the day. It was an ambitious walk, but I had to give it a try. Being that close to so many bodies, the stench was unbearable, and the flies were biting me left and right.

I carried a sense of hopefulness as I wandered at a steady, slow pace from the stadium grounds. Away from the river, away from the bodies. Each step made me feel more confident of finding someone—

no one would be near the area of the dead, and the further I went, the better my chances.

From driving down to the stadium and museum, I was familiar with a few of these streets, including some that I was always taught to avoid. It wasn't the best of neighborhoods.

There were plenty of empty lots and vacant buildings. The community college was located a few blocks from the stadium; I headed in that direction, knowing if there were people, they could be there.

If that was a bust, I'd keep going into the city.

After crossing through what seemed like an endless parking lot, I made it to a main street and saw the sign for the college.

I had to stop. Even though I had only made it several blocks, my legs were wobbly. I hadn't a clue how I was going to make it a mile into the city. Stopping and resting, I supposed, or happening upon people. I realized the latter wasn't truly a possibility when I started walking again.

There were absolutely no sounds. None. Just me. No animals or birds. Where were the birds? It was insane, how quiet it was. Scary too. I didn't lose focus; I kept my eyes peeled, just in case some horror novel did come true and vicious creatures suddenly flocked to me from every direction.

Nearly three weeks of my life had been lost; something huge had apparently occurred. Somehow, someway, it had been announced. Had it been decades earlier, I would have spotted one of those newspaper boxes and had an answer. But no one used those; they drew their information from handheld devices and the airwaves, whether it was television, radio or the Internet.

None of those were available. At least, not where I was.

A block ahead there were two fast food restaurants and a convenience store. The sight of them gave me energy, because they were a goal.

My duffle bag was heavy, dragging me down, but the big clothes and large clumpy boots I was wearing had to play a part in my difficulty walking. Getting something else to wear wasn't an option; there was nothing around.

Hobbling, I aimed for the convenience store. There had to be a trace of something. A newspaper, a magazine—hell, even a tabloid. As I drew closer I saw them—bodies. Not stacked and wrapped, but scattered about the store parking lot.

Not that my pace could have slowed down much more, but it did. How many were there? Eight? Ten? They were decomposing, and they looked different than the soldiers' bodies. These people had been shot.

I could only guess they were looters. My God, how long had the city been in despair before it just stopped?

Next door to the store was a McDonald's. The windows there, like the convenience store, were busted out. Who would want to loot a McDonald's? At first people probably went for the cash, then—which became clear as I stepped into the dark convenience store—they had grabbed anything.

Food. Water. Drinks. The shelves were bare. Absolutely nothing left. Not a candy bar, a can of soda … nothing save a few packs of cigarettes. That surprised me—and of course, I collected them. Why not take up smoking? It would pass time, and who cared if it killed me? There was a lighter on the counter, and I took it.

But I wasn't there for smokes, food or a drink. I was there for information.

The rack that held the newspapers was turned over, and a few papers were spilled on the floor. Most had been trampled on, scattered about by the people who had run in and out. There were magazines behind the counter. No one had touched those; most of them were pornographic.

Then I spotted the *Newsweek*. The cover image was a man in a simple cloth respiratory mask. I stepped over the newspaper rack and behind the counter, reaching for it. The headline read "Is Now the

Time for Prayer?" with a subheading of "ERDS claims millions in days."

ERDS?

The date on the magazine was April 24. Two days before the city was shut down. That magazine was my gold mine. Just flipping through, I saw the entire issue was dedicated to whatever this ERDS was. It wasn't something I could glance at; I needed to read it, and to do so, I needed to get out of the dark store and find a place to settle.

That magazine would give me answers.

Turning, my foot caught something, fanning it out and scattering its pages. A newspaper—the only one with an intact front page. I reached down and grabbed it.

It was a local paper dated the twenty-eighth, and it was the last one ever to have been printed and delivered in the city. The newspaper admitted such, because under edition it didn't say morning or afternoon, it said ... last. "Last Edition."

A story on the front page claimed, "City Struggles as Death Toll Reaches 80,000."

"Nowhere to Put the Dead."

The paper had come out not even two weeks after I fell unconscious in the bar. Two weeks, and that many bodies? Now I knew, because of the magazine and newspaper, that I was wrong in my thinking.

There was no one waiting on the other side of the bridge, no help outside the city. If I deduced it correctly, and at a glance I was pretty sure I did, it wasn't just the north side or my city—it was everywhere. The newspaper's bold, two-word headline said it all.

"It's Over!"

And it was.

10. ABSORPTION

I was numb.

Perhaps that was why I moved with such little concern for my physical well-being. Taking it all in as I pushed forward, I found myself oddly void of any emotions. Was it the shock of it all, or had I really shut down after the accident so much that I just didn't care?

I supposed some rest, food and educating myself with the magazine would clarify that.

Maybe.

I made it across the bridge into the downtown area of the city. Traffic was lined up on both sides; some vehicles were empty but most contained bodies, waiting to go somewhere as if life was better wherever they thought they were heading.

The bridge was blocked by abandoned military trucks. No soldiers; they'd left their posts, unlike Wilkes and Stevens.

While there may not have been people, there were certainly flies. It was creepy to think that the sole surviving species on the planet Earth was the common fly.

Feast and multiply. It scared me to imagine what would happen when they ran out of bodies.

I knew one thing for certain—I'd rest, and then I had to get out of the city as soon as possible. Not only was it overflowing with corpses, but it was a death trap. The diseases dead bodies carried alone were enough to set my sights on finding an exit solution.

I looked down at the Wilkes watch—it was nearly 2 p.m. It had taken me hours to make it a mile or so. I had to hunker down. Maybe the next day's light would give me enough energy to find my way home. Or at least closer.

There was a grand hotel that used to be one of the city's best near the river, only two blocks from the edge of the bridge. It was easy to spot and didn't seem damaged from behind. As I walked closer, I saw it was barricaded off. The streets around it were blocked with those horses and rapidly erected fences.

Keep Out

Military Personnel Only

I didn't see anyone though. Only bodies. More bodies, lots of bodies. Some weren't even covered. Just tossed on top of each other outside the fences, as if this were a garbage drop-off point.

As I crossed through the barricade around the hotel, it became apparent that it had been some sort of military setup, if only briefly.

Maybe a medical station. There were tents and trucks outside, and the main doors were open.

There were rows upon rows of cots set up in the huge lobby, but there were no bodies on them. No blankets. Only the remnants of illness left on the mattresses and a sour smell that filled the air.

Taking refuge on a lobby couch was out of the question; they had been cleared out.

But the gift shop was not. That made me happy.

There were three shops in the lobby, untouched by looters, and one of them had clothing. Anything was better than what I was wearing. Setting down my duffle bag, I went into the shop.

I was able to find some things, including underwear. The only thing I couldn't find was shoes. At least, shoes I could walk in. They had sandals and flats, but I couldn't see me click-clacking my way down the barren streets. The boots weren't going to cut it. I was in a hotel, there had to be something here. There were tons of bodies outside; I quickly dismissed the idea of looking for shoes on one of them. Remembering how my hand had sunk into flesh, I could only imagine what was going to be in those shoes.

No, the hotel was my answer.

I thought getting into the rooms would be difficult, considering the keycard system, but then Christine came to mind again. I made a mental note that I was going to try to find out what had happened to her and her family.

She had worked at a hotel for years, and had told me that all the keys systems were run on a triple-A battery setup. There was also a master key for emergency workers. If I needed to, I'd look for that.

I didn't feel much like going through each room like Charlton Heston in *The Omega Man*. I only needed shoes. So I headed behind the front desk and into the offices located there.

Something, somewhere.

But that was a bust. I checked every drawer, thinking some secretary or accounting clerk would have had an extra pair of shoes.

My feet ached, and my ankles hurt from the weight of the combat boots. I stopped for a moment, sat on the chair behind the front desk and took a second to think. It was funny, because I could have just stopped, found a place to hunker down, read my magazine and relax, but I couldn't until I found what I needed.

After gathering my bearings and smoking a cigarette, coughing with every puff, I ventured further into the hotel.

It was a hotel, for crying out loud—I had to find what I needed.

<><><><>

My original assessment of the hotel—that it would be like the magazine, a gold mine—was correct. I didn't have to go further than the first floor.

A simple walk-through of the dark kitchen led me to a back hall that joined every cooking or catering department and eventually an employee lounge.

Her name was J. Cooke, and I found a decent pair of sneakers in her locker. There were shoes in other lockers, mostly work shoes, but hers fit me. I thanked her.

A back storage closet gave me not only a better flashlight, but a pillow and blanket. I didn't need to go up to the rooms after all.

I noted that the pool area had a hot tub, still filled with water not clouded over. I'd probably use that for cleanup the next day. Who knew the next time I'd get to do that.

I returned one more time to the kitchen for water and cereal, then settled in the corner of the first-floor lounge for the remainder of the day and night.

A private setup, probably for parties, it had three couches and a set of "pull close" doors for privacy. I gathered every little table lantern I could find—the tiny ones with a single wick, oil based, that were used more for decoration than real lighting—taking them from the lounge and two restaurants. Alone they were a mere flicker, but thirty of them together lit the room.

At least that night wouldn't be spent in the dark. If I didn't catch on fire.

There were no windows in my corner, so I couldn't see what was going on outside. That helped with me not being scared.

Following my criminal behavior of breaking into the locked liquor cabinet under the bar, I settled for the night with a bottle of whiskey, MRE spaghetti, fruit ring cereal and *Newsweek*.

11. ERDS

I knew I'd rest easy that night, since neither the magazine nor paper made mention of the rising dead, cannibalistic creatures or rage monsters. They wouldn't jump at me from a corner. Nor would crazed survivors.

While I'd fallen into what was probably an alcohol-induced coma, the world had ended.

The nice thing about journalism was the recap of news just in case someone missed it. Yeah, someone did.

Newsweek had plenty of articles; the entire magazine was dedicated to it.

ERDS. European Respiratory Distress Syndrome.

It had started in Europe in February. I hadn't known, hadn't paid any attention, because my own world was ending. No one knew where it came from or what started it.

One article suggested that Mother Nature just said, "Enough." I wasn't knowledgeable enough about viruses to know what sounded right or wrong. I hadn't followed the story, obviously, so I had to rely on the magazine as if it were some sort of history book. My only source of education.

In February, in the middle of cold and flu season, it began as a different strain. "H" something, "N" something. Those who fell victim died from complications. It showed no prejudice. The ill didn't need to be old or young or have any serious health problems. To quote one of the doctors interviewed, "If you get it, you die."

A one hundred percent kill rate.

But the people weren't getting it as easily as the ordinary flu. I read that in the beginning it was one in a thousand that caught that particular strain. Then it progressed, and one in a thousand people caught ERDS, whether they'd had a case of the flu or not, or even a shot. Then …

One in five hundred.

One in a hundred.

By the middle of April, one in two.

By the time the article was printed, Europe was done, and the ERDS strain was spreading like wildfire. The early phase of high communicability made it easy for it to cross continents.

What started as a sniffle cascaded to full-blown pneumonia symptoms, people choking and drowning on their own overproduction of phlegm. That was if the fever didn't kill them.

It was inhumane. People suffered at first for nearly a week, then, as healthcare facilities became unable to handle all the ill, as medicine, antiviral and fever-reducer stockpiles plummeted, the sick weren't getting their symptoms treated, and the symptoms killed them faster.

That was at the end—what I gathered from that last newspaper article.

My city was done. Officials had told families to place their dead out like garbage. However, I guess, soon enough those caring for the ill just got sick themselves.

My head was spinning from all the information I was trying to process, along with the alcohol. It was a long time since alcohol had affected me. Maybe I shouldn't have drunk, especially after alcohol nearly killed me, but I didn't care.

Why should I?

ERDS was hailed as the extinction event. Not just humans, but everything. Every species carried it and contracted it. Birds dropped from the sky, dogs died in the street.

Everything but flies.

Scientists never found one occurrence of immunity. Not one case? What was I? A fluke, or did I really get it and I was that one in eight billion that beat it?

Extinction event. Everyone, everything, died.

Except for me.

Was that possible? It couldn't be. There was no way, no how. I was the only one remaining. There had to be a mistake in the article; perhaps the author died before he or she knew people could beat it.

I stood and started blowing out the lanterns. I'd leave one on; that wasn't a fire hazard.

A few articles remained unread; I saved them for another time. I managed to find a package of something called Pain Away in the employee first aid cabinet. I washed those down and finished off my bottle of water to thwart any post-drinking soreness. My previous headache had finally subsided; I didn't need another.

If anything, that whiskey would help me sleep. My body was tired and achy, my mind and heart heavy.

Not wanting to think of anything else, I closed my eyes and prayed for a dreamless sleep.

12. THE DREAM

It was the same one. It always was. At first it was every night, then just every time I dreamed.

The phone call. The knock. The scream. My scream.

That day was forever embedded in my mind.

"Nearly done," I said to my husband on the phone.

I had been working all Saturday morning on marketing reports. That was my job. I collected the research from the study groups and compiled it.

"We won't be much longer. Unless you want us to stay out," he said.

"No. Come home."

"Daddy, can we stop and get pizza?" I heard my six-year-old daughter ask from the back seat. I laughed.

"Well, Faye, you heard Sammy. She wants to stop."

"Rich …"

"We won't be long, enjoy your break."

"How's Mark doing?"

"Oh, he's a champ. If his driver's test was today he'd pass with flying colors. He's excellent."

"Hey, Mom!" Mark called from the background.

"Drive," Rich told him. "And remember—two seconds after the light changes."

"Yep. Got it."

I laughed. "Well, get back to being driving instructor. I'll see you soon."

"Sounds good. Love you."

"Love you, too." I pulled the phone from my ear, but not before I heard an eerie "Oh my God" from Rich.

The line went dead.

It didn't sit well with me. Immediately, I tried to call him back. It went directly to voice mail.

How long and how many times did I call, text, both Rich's phone and Mark's? It wasn't more than an hour and a half, because the knock came at the door.

One police officer. "Mrs. Wills?"

My family had been killed. My entire family, in one single instant. Even after my son hesitated to go when the light turned green, a truck going fifty miles an hour ran a red light and rammed right into my family's car.

The impact sent the car sailing down a busy street. I wasn't the only one who lost that afternoon. Like a billiard ball, it rolled and ricocheted into other vehicles.

For the first few days, after the shock, I struggled with the fact of what my family had endured. I was crushed over the thought of my poor daughter in the back seat screaming out for help.

The only comfort came from the coroner, who said they all died on impact. He said they didn't suffer. But his report wasn't enough. I actually sought him out.

"Swear to me."

"Mrs. Wills, this is highly unusual."

"Swear to me, please. Swear to me on anything that's important. Please, swear to me they didn't suffer."

He gripped my hand, looked me in the eye. "On my own child, I swear to you."

It took everything I had not to kill myself in the days following the funeral. Aside from being cowardly, I wanted to see it through. I wanted to see justice delivered to the man who not only took my family, but destroyed the lives of four other families in the process.

I sat through every day, every hour of that trial. Eight counts of vehicular homicide while under the influence. He had no defense and begged to be put away. I listened as he said he had no will, he was drunk, and that the day it happened he had buried his own three-year-old son, who had passed away from leukemia.

When the families stood up and asked the judge to deliver a life sentence, I saw a man who was remorseful. Putting him away wasn't bringing back my family. He wasn't a man who was tossing his actions aside; he would definitely live and carry what he'd done for the rest of his life. That was punishment enough. I told the judge that.

It didn't matter. When the judge handed down the sentence of twenty-five years, I left the courtroom, went home, threw away my car keys and started drinking. I didn't stop. Not until the day I dropped unconscious in that bar, only to wake up to a nightmare world.

Thing was, even before the flu, I was living in a nightmare world.

The dream would never stop; it would ease, but never go away.

I was pretty sure I screamed when I sprang awake. I always did. I'd wake in a sweat, heart beating, and then cry.

Not this morning. I didn't cry. For the first time since it had happened, I realized *why* it had happened. They were spared the madness that I now had to experience. I had already grieved for them; I still was, and would be for a long time.

They were all I had in the world, and their loss was bigger to me than what I faced now.

My losses were tallied long before the world keeled over.

All that was left for me to do was to get out of the city and try to make my way to my house. What I would do after that remained to be seen.

The Wilkes watch read a little after 8 a.m. It was time to gather my things and get moving.

My first focus was accomplished—I'd found out what had happened to the world. Focus two was the hotel and the answer to what had happened to all the people. Now I just wanted to get to my final focus, and that was simply to get home.

13. SQUEAKY WHEEL

I did several things before leaving that hotel. I cleaned up, put on comfortable clothing and transferred items from that damn bulky duffle bag to a large suitcase with wheels. That suitcase was packed. I grabbed anything and everything I thought I might use in my journey home. I carried a small sack over my shoulder with my day's rations. How long I'd be out and how far I'd get would be down to my health—which felt remarkably better. I didn't feel as weak, and those shoes were going to work.

From what I could see, the main streets were free of traffic, except for the sidewalks lined with bodies that had occasionally tumbled into the road. But in the back of my mind, I had it figured that the main roads out of town were going to be jammed or blocked. The fleeting thought to grab a car left me.

I had to walk. It wasn't going to be so hard now—at least, that's what I believed. I was wearing better shoes and I wasn't carrying that heavy duffle bag. Pulling something on wheels would be a lot easier. However, it was much more annoying.

One of those wheels squeaked.

The concrete jungle of the city was a cavern for echoing. Each step I took, the wheel squealed and bounced back at me, over and over.

"Are you kidding me?" I said. "The entire city and I get *the* bad suitcase. Unreal."

I grew more irritated with each step. I suppose there were other things that could have annoyed me, and perhaps the noisy suitcase was just a distraction to keep my mind off it all.

It was better when I got onto the expressway that went around the city. The noise of the squeaky wheel was still there, still loud, but it carried out in the wind and didn't echo back at me. My plan was to follow the expressway until the end of the city and go south. At some point they had to have stopped blocking the roads and bridges, or so I thought. Cars were crammed into some sections of the roads, then there would be a long stretch of nothing.

Nothing except that damn squeaky wheel. I think I stopped every twenty feet to get a break from it.

The expressway was also named River Trail Road, because at times it ran alongside the river. In some places it rose high above other roadways, giving me a good view of all that had gone down.

I wondered how a flu so feral, how something so swift, had left enough well people around for long enough to loot and cause such damage. Stores had been broken into, glass busted. The bullet-strewn victims were easy to spot, as opposed to the people who had died of the flu. With something that had wiped out so many people, I would imagine I'd be too sick to want to steal.

Then it dawned on me. The city had been shut down a week before I woke up. Those last few days of chaos and fear—my God, how people must have panicked, knowing it was over. How scared they must have been. It wouldn't take long for thousands of people to destroy a city. People fighting, because all they had left to fight for was a morsel of food and their last dying breath. Maybe they'd held out hope that they'd be spared. Or maybe they were spared, and had been shot while looting, or even because they weren't sick.

That thought struck me. What if that had happened to me? What if someone sick and bitter had known I wasn't going to get the flu and said, "The hell with her, why does that drunk deserve to live?"—then tagged me as dead?

How many people might have been that tiny speck of hope, but were extinguished by another?

I would never know.

I could only guess. That passed the time as I walked slowly, tugging along my squeaky case, darting in and out of cars, and when there weren't cars, avoiding the massive amount of dead birds that lay about everywhere.

Taking in the sights of destroyed properties and bridges to nowhere.

There was something awesome about the sight of the main bridges. It wasn't so much the bridges themselves that had been destroyed as it was the ramps leading onto them, which had been set with some sort of explosive. The biggest bridge was breathtaking, the ramps folded like a house of cards.

It was as good a place to stop as any. I'd actually done really well, making it to the edge of the city. Some water, a cigarette, maybe a cracker. It was warm on the roadway, the sun beating down and a constant light breeze sweeping in and blowing out waves of stench. I pushed down the handle on my suitcase and sat down.

Had the world been normal, had there even been birds, I probably wouldn't have either noticed or heard them. But like the squeaky wheel, the sound carried to me. In fact, it scared the hell out of me, and I jolted.

It sounded like a big hollow rubber ball smacking against a concrete wall. But it wasn't just one bounce; it echoed loudly.

Had something dropped? Was it my imagination?

Slowly I stood. It was quiet. Just as I was dismissing it and had started to sit again, I heard the same bouncing sound. I jumped back to my feet. Determining where it was coming from was hard, because of the echoes in the empty city.

I was also above the town. Where? Where was it coming from?

The binoculars were in my rations bag, which sat next to the suitcase. I bent down for it, and heard another sound. This one was frantic, metal against metal. In my mind I immediately envisioned gang members, wearing bandanas, carrying weapons. Men turned beasts in an apocalyptic world, no law and order. Ravage. Pillage.

Listening to the metallic clashing, my fear increased. They were coming for me. Taunting me, running a pipe against a fence, because that's what it sounded like. The same pipe they would probably use to bash my skull in after they robbed me.

I wasn't sticking around. I was in the open. How foolish. How stupid I'd been to believe I was alone. If I lived, someone else did, and they weren't necessarily nice.

I gathered up my rations bag, tossed it over my shoulder, popped up the handle on my suitcase and bolted.

The pipe against the fence stopped. My God, they'd spotted me. The faster I ran, the louder and higher-pitched the suitcase squealed. I was a moving target, easy to hear. My heart pounding, barely able to breathe, I dropped the suitcase.

The moment I did, the moment I started to run, I heard something else. Something I didn't expect.

A voice. A male voice, deep, raspy and not young. It screamed out, cracking. "Hey! I hear you! Hey! Is someone there! Anyone! Help!"

I stopped running.

14. HELLO

It took only a moment after the voice stopped calling for me to believe I had completely lost my mind. I'd read the magazine; I knew the numbers. While I was surely delusional to believe everyone that had survived would be nice—really? A gang?

Shaking my head at my own silly fantasy, one brought on by silence, I walked back to my suitcase. I was certain the noises, the voices, were like a mirage of water in the desert.

But ... what if?

As crazy as it seemed, I took a deep breath and called out. "Hello!"

My voice bounced back at me.

Quiet.

"Hello!"

I knew immediately that it wasn't *my* voice. One would think I should be ecstatic—I mean, I'd woken up to an extinction-level event, it was the third day after waking, and it was the first human contact I'd had.

I wasn't. I was actually kind of scared.

Unable to pinpoint where the voice had come from, I turned clockwise, searching. Wherever he'd called from, it had reverberated. But how far away was he? In the silent, dead city, sound traveled.

For a second, I thought about leaving. Chalking it up to my imagination again.

"Hello?" he called out.

"Why are you hiding?" I shouted back.

"What?"

"I said ..." I sucked in a huge breath. "Why are you hiding?"

"I'm stuck!"

"Is this a trap?"

"Lady, please!"

"Fine! Where are you?"

A pause.

"Jail."

Jail? Was he kidding? I slowly looked to my right. I stood on the roadway directly in front of the county jail property. The red-brick, multi-building complex was close, yet a long walk because I was on the overpass.

To get to the jail I'd have to backtrack. It wasn't going to be an easy trek. But if he was indeed there, and stuck, then it would be inhumane to keep walking and not at least try to help him.

15. LOCKED IN

Before I made it from the rise of the overpass to street level, I called out once more to ask where I could find him. I knew full well that I probably wouldn't hear him once I was on the street.

His voice cracked horribly from yelling. He said something like "Building One, Two B." I had no clue what that meant.

The county jail was near the city's judicial building. I had never been there, not even for a traffic ticket, so I was going in blind.

When I left the overpass, I glanced at my Wilkes watch. It was shortly before noon. By the time I'd finally lugged my belongings and myself to the city building, it was pushing one o'clock. Not that I was moving that slowly; I just didn't know where I was going. I suppose he'd thought I'd left him. The suitcase wheel was squeaking loudly again, all the more so in the more confined space of the city.

Finally I worked out where I was going, and it was evident that toward the end it had been a complete madhouse.

Police cars had been burned, bodies were everywhere, military posts once again set up and abandoned. I wondered how the man calling me was stuck when the front doors were busted open, numerous bodies of men wearing bright orange jumpsuits scattered across the pavement.

I brought in my suitcase, but left it just inside the entrance of the building labeled number one. I pulled out the hefty flashlight. While there were some small windows, very little light made its way in. The building I sought was clearly numbered, located on the river-facing portion of the property.

In a sense I was proud of myself for being brave; I never really was. I didn't do haunted houses or go to see scary movies unless I was with a group of people. Yet I made it into the building and followed the signs.

Doors were open everywhere, and the stench of death filled the air. A map on the wall just outside a room marked "Visitor Waiting Room" told me that area 2B was on the second floor.

I searched for a stairwell, and when I found one it was even darker than the rest of the building. Pitch black. I was thankful for my flashlight, but I was still cautious, my mind flashing back to scary movies. I stayed close to the wall, hoping some sick, flu-stricken man wouldn't grab my ankles and ask me to come have chicken with him.

Second floor.

Again, another unlocked door. The stairs led to a hall, which in turn led to a huge, open control room.

There was a body of a guard sitting at the control board, surrounded by blank monitors. Still, he was only the third person in authority I'd seen holding their post.

In the hall outside the control room I could see marks on the walls. I stopped at 2A and aimed the beam of my light through the small glass window on the metal door.

"Hello!" I called.

"I hear you!"

I moved to 2B. The door was the same, closed; I could see some light through the window, but not much. I walked to the door and pulled. It was locked, of course.

I lifted my flashlight and leaned to the window to peek in.

My beam caught a pair of eyes, the light reflecting from them and making them appear a glowing green, and I jumped back with a scream.

"Thank God." His voice was muffled, more so than it had been when I was on the street and heard him calling out.

I inched to the door. I couldn't see much of him, only that he was hunched over and looking through the window at me.

"I am so happy to see you!" He sounded excited. "I am so glad to see you. I heard you."

I couldn't see much of his face. I was scared; after all, this man was in jail.

"Are you a murderer?" I asked.

"What? No. I …"

"A rapist?"

"No."

"Child molester?"

"Lady. No. I'm on the second floor."

"What does that have to do with it?"

"Lower the floor, the lower the risk."

I realize it was stupid; I was face to face, sort of, with another survivor, but I was hesitant. Was I going to help this man, only to be slaughtered?

"Is that true?"

"Think about it. Even if it wasn't, would I tell you?"

I didn't like the sound of his voice. It was husky, for lack of a better word. Worn and dry, deep and not youthful. There were years of experience in it, years of hardship.

"Please, I'll tell you anything you need to know. Let me out."

I reached for the door and pulled. "It's locked."

"Can you shoot at it? Maybe that will break the lock?"

"Shoot at it with what?"

"Your gun."

"I don't have a gun." I cringed. Why would I tell him that?

"All that shit that happened out there, you're wandering around without a gun for protection?"

"Everyone's dead."

"I'm not. You're not. Others are not."

"I can't get you out. It's locked, see." I pulled. "Sorry. I am. I don't know what to do." I turned.

"Wait!" he shouted. "Where are you going?"

"I'm sorry, I can't get you out. I have to go."

"Stop." He banged on the door. "Don't leave. There are keys."

I stopped walking.

"Please. I can't believe you're gonna leave."

Slowly, I turned around. "Where? Where are the keys?"

"The locks on these doors are manual override. There's a black box in the control room. They're in there—or, if you can, find a guard."

"There's a dead guard in there." I pointed backwards.

"He may have keys."

I held up my hand. "I'll check."

"Thank you."

It was frightening. I was talking to a mere eye with a voice attached. I didn't know what kind of man would emerge from behind door 2B. If I freed him, I wasn't sticking around long enough to find out. My good deed was to release him.

If he was in jail, he was obviously dangerous.

I returned to the control room and the dead guard. One hand covering my nose, I reached down to pat his sides. Nothing. No keys. Before I gave up, I lifted him from his slumped position. Decomposition had nearly glued his face to the counter. I gagged.

I was already in a weakened state, tired again, my legs wearing down, my body lacking energy, and hoisting him back seemed to rob me of what little I had left.

Brackenridge. There was a tag on his uniform. T. Brackenridge.

Then I remembered—he was more than a body. "I'm sorry, T," I whispered.

There was a huge key ring attached to the front loop of his pants. I undid them and lifted the keys. Nothing was marked clearly, and there had to be at least thirty of them. But for the man behind that steel door, I'd try each one.

I jingled the keys as I approached the door and heard him cheer happily. Tucking the flashlight under my arm to shine on the lock, I began the process of elimination. Jail man stayed close, talking to me as I tried each key.

"I heard the squeaking," he said. "It was the first sound in days."

Key tried … failed. Another tried … failed.

"It was far away at first and then moved closer."

I didn't speak, just kept trying the keys. I didn't want to lose track of the ones I'd already attempted.

"I was able to see you moving from the one window. Then I waited until the squeaking stopped so I could make some noise, or else you wouldn't hear me."

Another key, another failed attempt. I didn't think any of them would work.

"We have an open rec area—it's open air. I figured if you could hear me from anywhere, it would be there."

I grunted in frustration. Why wouldn't any of the keys work?

"Thank you for stopping. Thank you for coming. I've been here for almost two weeks. I think."

I shook my head, still focused on the keys.

"I lost track of time. The one guard unlocked the cells and the open rec, but not this POD door. Everyone kept dying. I thought …"

Key in.

"I thought I was gonna die." He chuckled. "I still may …"

Click.

"Oh my God," he gasped.

The door unlocked and, slightly fearful, I pulled it open.

Not only was I pelted by a strong, sour aroma, I was also slammed by the large man who barreled out and immediately embraced me. He hugged me as if I were a long-lost friend he hadn't seen in years. I was smothered in his arms.

"Thank you," he said, and stepped back. He placed his hands on my face and kissed my forehead. "Thank you so much." He hugged me again.

"You're welcome." I pulled away and took a good look at him. He could have been a poster representation of a biker group or professional wrestling organization. He was tall and bulky, strong looking. He was bald, his face tough with overgrown whiskers that had probably once been a goatee. He had to be in his forties—late forties, maybe. The top portion of his orange jumpsuit hung down to his waist and he used the sleeves as a belt.

He was staring at me.

"Do you need water, food?" I asked.

"Yeah, water. I've been rationing what I had."

I reached into my bag and handed him a water bottle. He took it, sipped gratefully yet sparingly, then handed it back.

"Keep it," I told him, and turned, aiming the flashlight ahead of me. "The building is pretty dark, so follow me. Do you need anything before we get outside?"

"No. No, I'm sure I can find what I need out there."

I agreed with a simple nod, leading the way past the control room and to the stairwell. Admittedly, the stairs were a lot less spooky with him behind me.

We emerged and I faced him. "How long since you've been outside?"

"I was tossed in here right after the shutdown. I'm guessing nearly two weeks."

"Just be prepared, okay?"

"I can only imagine."

"No, you can't."

At the entrance, I grabbed my suitcase by the handle and started toting it along.

"The squeaky wheel," he said with a slight smile. "That saved me."

"Yeah." I exhaled. "You sure you don't need anything?"

"No."

"You should be able to find whatever you need. Some of the stores were looted, but the businesses and stuff probably have machines." I stepped outside and watched as he covered his eyes. The sun was obviously blinding him. "You okay?"

"Yeah, just tough to see. I've been in the dark a while."

"Let your eyes adjust. And ... Are you sure I can't give you an MRE or box of cereal to tide you over?"

"Tide me over until when?"

"Until you find food."

"I'm confused." He lifted his arms. "If you have food, why am I ... Wait. Wait. No one is around. Everyone is gone. We're not sticking together? You're going your own way?"

"No, actually, I'm headed home."

"What the hell, lady! Why pull me out then?"

"You asked."

"You're serious?" he asked with a hint of disbelief. "I'm not going to walk with you?"

After a second's pause, I simply shook my head. "No." Tugging my squeaky wheeled suitcase behind me, I slowly moved onward.

16. DODGE

My Wilkes watch reminded me it was May seventh when I glanced down to check the time as I walked from the jail. It was nearly two. That meant I'd lost two hours of travel. I'd gone eight blocks out of my way to backtrack to the jail, and I had to go those eight blocks again to return to the main expressway.

Something good had come out of it; I'd been able to help someone who would have otherwise starved and died in that building. Actually, his name was William Cash. But—as he'd informed me as we walked through the jail—people had called him Dodge since he was sixteen years old. I didn't ask why.

It was time to move forward. I had to keep going if I wanted to make it further south and get some distance before the sun started to set.

The temperatures would drop without the sun, and with no power, no street lights, it would be too dark to travel. Plus, I needed to find shelter while I could still see.

I had fully intended on going alone, but ten steps down the street, I stopped. Was I insane? I didn't know what was ahead of me, if more people were alive, if things were going to get dangerous or even if I'd ever see another living human being again. Having spent so much time alone and withdrawn after the accident had made me numb to the world. It wasn't fair to Dodge to walk away, nor was it smart of me.

I turned and, with a sigh, signaled a half-assed wave for him to join me.

I didn't know much about Dodge—actually, nothing at all. I figured I would find out on our journey.

He was a talker. He was also something else, which I learned right away—he was resourceful.

Not twenty feet further, he stopped and said, "Wait up."

"What's wrong?"

"That wheel, it was all well and fine to let me know you were coming, but I think that might drive me nuts."

"It will. But what can we do? Transfer the stuff out?"

"Nah." He shook his head and walked over to an abandoned police car. He popped the hood.

I joined him. "What are you doing?"

"Fixing that wheel." He emerged from under the hood with the car's dip stick and went back to the suitcase. He crouched down and began to wipe the oil from the stick onto the problematic wheel. "Nudge it back and forth for me."

"Oh my God, that is really smart," I said.

"Not really. The squeaky wheel gets the oil. I had a friend, Jack Hanson, who used to say that." He stood with a grunt, his knees cracking. "Try it, see if it needs more."

I pushed the suitcase back and forth. "Wow, it's great. Thank you."

"Now, will you let me tote that for you?" He reached out for it. "It's the least I can do."

I surrendered the suitcase; even with the ease of wheeling it, it was heavy.

"Good Lord, what do you have in this?"

"A lot of stuff. We'll need it."

"Yeah, I guess with the city shutting down first, pickings are slim. That will change when we move further out. I hope."

"Me too." I walked alongside him at a steady but comfortable pace.

"Tell me again," he said, "where are we going?"

"I wanna go home. Downing Park."

He nodded. "Not a bad place. About three miles from where I live."

"Do you need to find your home?"

He hesitated before answering, then with a sigh, said, "No. No, I'd rather not. Not yet."

I was going to ask why, but refrained. The shake to his voice told me he'd explain when he was ready. It wasn't my place to ask. Of course, he wasn't shy about asking me questions.

"Why are we headed north into town if we need to go south? Not that I'm griping—I'm just curious."

"Because it's easier to walk the expressway. Even with the road-blocks, it's a straight shot, but to get back to the expressway we have to go this way. Unfortunately. And my plan is to keep going south until we find a bridge that hasn't been destroyed."

"Yeah, I heard those."

I glanced at him.

"The day they did it." He shrugged. "Was really the thing that nailed the reality of it for me. Just hearing it. The concrete falling, explosions. You could see it on the television, but to be right there, right near it. Hard to explain." He took a deep breath. "So why don't we just take the side streets? The expressways may be a straight shot, but they aren't a straight way through."

"You mean walk the side streets? Kind of a longer way, don't you think?"

"No, I mean drive. We may have to foot it over a bridge, but at least drive until we get there. Take the side streets in and out. I know the area well."

"How are we supposed to drive?"

"A car, hopefully one that didn't run out of gas while waiting."

I laughed at that. "I'm sure we'll just find a set of keys in a car."

"Um … yeah." He pointed to one; the door was open, and there was a decomposing body inside. "Keys."

"Let me rephrase that. A car with keys and no body."

"Just take the body out," Dodge suggested.

"Go on." I nodded. "Touch it. Try to move it."

He reached into the car, then paused and glanced at me. "Why? What's gonna happen?"

"Not like the movies. Go on. Hollywood made me delusional as well."

He braved it up, covered his mouth and nose as he reached in. I watched him grab the body, and then the big, tough man from jail squealed in disgust, jumped back and rubbed his hands frantically on the sides of his jumpsuit.

"Whatever happens to the body," I said, "it just eats through the fabric. It's gross."

"I heard something about that once. I didn't think it was real. They said the body, when decomposing, can be like an acid when it breaks down."

"From what I saw, that's real."

He peered down at his hands, playing with a substance between his fingers. "Feels like gooey honey."

I blinked a few times. "I'll never eat honey again."

"Got news for you—fresh honey may not be an option anymore, unless you find some bees."

"Here." I reached into my pocket and handed him the tiny bottle of sanitizer. "Use that."

"Thanks." He squirted a lot on his hands and looked around as he rubbed them together. "Okay, so, key in the car probably means body in the car. So we have to find a moveable, working car, preferably a couple years old."

"What's the age have to do with it?"

"A lot." He looked around as we walked on, peeking into every car, occasionally stopping to try a handle. He commented on some that were perfect but had no gas, or complained because there was a body or two in them. Finally, just as we hit the traffic leading up to what I knew was a hospital, Dodge clapped his hands together. He let go of the suitcase and walked over to a car.

"What are you doing?"

"Abandoned." He indicated the open door. "And I can pull this on the sidewalk, cut through that lot there and down the street." He reached in and popped the trunk, walked around to the back of the car and started rummaging.

He smiled, then cheered and lifted out a small gray case. "Cheap, but it works—roadside kit."

I shook my head, confused, as he climbed into the car and lay down. His feet extended out through the door. "Dodge?"

He grunted. "Give me a second."

"Dodge."

"I don't wanna walk. This car has gas."

Just as I was about to call his name again, the car started. "You jumped it."

"If that's what you want to call it." He slid out. "Once we stop we may not be able to restart it. But we can find another." He walked to the suitcase and grabbed it. "Getting in?"

"How did you know to do that?"

"My job."

"Ah." I nodded. "You were a car thief."

"What? A mechanic. A good one, too. Been doing it since I was a kid. Hence my teenage nickname." He tossed the suitcase in the car. "Dodge."

"Okay."

"Back in the day I could fix any Dodge. Trucks especially."

Suddenly his nickname made sense. It wasn't criminal related, like "Dodge the bullet" or "Get out of Dodge"—he fixed cars. Another reason I was glad to have him with me.

Thanking him, I got into the car. To me it didn't matter how many things he banged into getting off the street, or how many curbs he ran over. He was driving, and I was exceptionally glad to not be walking.

17. THE EMPTY CHAIR

We had to abandon ship. The comfort of the car, the silence of no conversation—with the exception of Dodge telling me to hold on when we had to run around or over something. Six miles into our trip, we hit an impassable section of road. Cars were jammed together like a parking lot. There was no getting around it. It began several dozen blocks before the area's teaching hospital. We should have known better.

But we made it six miles.

"Hate to say it, but we're probably gonna have to walk to a doable bridge. Then once we cross, find transportation," Dodge said. "Sorry I let you down. I really thought we'd get further.'

"Hey, we made it six miles. That was a lot of walking we saved. No, I expected to have to walk."

"We need to plan a course of action. Gotta see where we're going. How about you start checking these cars for a map? I'll trudge up to the overpass and take a look, maybe see if we can spot an upcoming bridge that looks good?"

"We can both go. I'm not that slow, am I?"

"No, that's not it. Just … I'll run it and run back. You settle. Maybe not move so much. We also gotta find a place to stop for the night."

"How about this? We both go—"

"How about not."

I turned to him, exasperated. "What's the problem?"

He placed his hands on his hips, lowered his head and looked down at me. "Honest?"

"Please."

"You don't … You don't look that well. You're pale." He reached up and touched my forehead in some sort of fatherly fashion. "You're cold and dry."

"Oh my God."

"No, Faye. If you are it, if you are the last person I have to talk to on this earth, I sure as shit ain't letting you drop from dehydration, exhaustion or whatever it is you are dealing with right now. Don't be a martyr."

It had taken getting into that car and being driven to realize I still wasn't anywhere near a hundred percent. I'd pushed it because I had to, when the truth was my body had been deprived of food and water for longer than I knew. Rest was what I needed, but instead I'd made things worse by constantly moving. I hadn't realized how weak I was until I didn't have to be quite so strong.

"You're right. I'm not well."

"I figured."

"It's not the flu."

"I kinda figured that too."

We stood there staring at each other in the midst of the mass of car congestion, trying to come up with a plan—and then we found a compromise.

The expressway was about a quarter mile from where we stood. We could walk around, find a place to rest, then after daybreak, trudge to the expressway. Or just go there now and make camp.

I didn't have a problem with making camp for the night on the road; Dodge did, but agreed as long as I'd take it easy when we got up there.

We headed in the direction of the expressway—to me that was the better place. We wouldn't have to waste energy getting there in the morning; we'd already be at our starting point.

Plus it gave a good view of the other side of the river. If there was any inkling of life, there would be an inkling of light and we'd see it in the dark world.

The sky was clear, and I suspected it wouldn't rain; a star-filled sky made for a brighter night.

Dodge kept checking every car he could for a map. I didn't believe he'd find one, because everyone used GPS. He said *he* didn't, which meant someone else might not rely on technology either.

Why did he need a map anyhow?

Sure enough, though, he found an atlas in the front door pocket of an older SUV.

He also made a point of stopping at an abandoned and apparently raided ambulance. All the medicine was gone, but there was a blanket.

The ramp to the road was packed with cars. Once we got past that and around the standard military blockade, we faced an empty stretch of road. Empty until the next exit ramp onto the road, where there were more trucks along with some cars. Lots of them. I wondered if they'd broken the barricade.

"It stopped there." Dodge pointed. "End of the city limits, at least far enough away from the hospitals and city. Bet Folsom Street Bridge is clear and we can walk across."

"I hope you're right."

"Once we get situated, I'll trudge up with the binoculars and take that look. Got enough strength to make it nearer to those cars?"

I did, and I told him so, but like it had two days before, my strength left me quickly. I was indeed ready to drop. I know it was a total of a mile walking, but to me, in my state, it could have been ten. I'd done too much the previous days.

As we approached the military trucks, Dodge said, "Let's stop here, this is as good a place as any."

I immediately stopped and dropped down to sit on the concrete. It had absorbed the sun and felt warm. We were near enough that if some freak storm rolled in we could jump into the back of the truck.

"Don't sit on the ground. Here." Dodge tossed the blanket my way.

I lifted my rear end and tucked the blanket under.

"I'll be back. Drink plenty of water," Dodge instructed, and then he darted off.

I hated it. I hated the fact that he looked at me like he had to take care of me. More than that, I hated the fact that I accepted the help.

He didn't stop, despite the fact that I had. Before the sun went down, he'd ripped out a bench seat from a minivan and another seat from some other car. I took the bench seat.

He built a small fire and instructed me to keep it going. Then he went off again.

Each return trip he'd drop off items, then leave again. Before he left the final time, he propped up two MREs close to the fire to warm them.

When he came back he was wearing baggy jeans almost too big for him and a flannel shirt. Dodge wasn't a small man. The man who'd unknowingly donated the clothes must have been huge. For some reason, the flannel shirt worked for him, as if it matched a personality I didn't know much about.

"Got you a new, non-squeaky case. Might wanna transfer." He sat down across the fire from me with an empty duffle bag. "I want to start packing some of the things I found."

He stared rummaging through his pile. I didn't know what he'd found, but he did toss a bottle of Ibuprofen my way. "Here, hold on to those."

"What did you gather?" I asked.

"I just grabbed. I'll sort through it all. What else do I have to do? I got you a jacket though."

"Why are you being so nice? Were you always such a nice guy?"

"I like to think I was." He shrugged. "Plus, you know, you saved my life. You really did. I owe ya."

"No, you don't."

"Yeah, I do. So, no arguments. The Chinese say something like, when you save a life you are responsible for that life. That means you gotta make sure I make right decisions. My right decision right now is making sure you're okay. You look better."

"I feel better. I haven't moved in hours."

"Maybe that's what you needed. Now, can you start transferring what you have in that suitcase, because I'm pretty curious to see what you've been tugging along."

I smiled slightly and pulled the suitcase closer. I unzipped it, and the first things I pulled out were two bottles.

"Drink much?" he said.

"Yep. If I can't handle the apocalypse, I might as well be drunk enough to ignore it."

He laughed when I handed him a bottle. "Can't beat this—dinner in a foil pouch and bourbon." Carefully, he grabbed the end of the MRE and slid it my way. "Watch, it's hot."

I took it, but just held on to it; I'd eat it in a bit. "How'd you end up in jail, Dodge? Do you mind me asking?"

"Nope, don't mind you asking at all. I shouldn't have been there. I should have been with my kids."

"Oh, you have children."

"Had. They caught the flu."

"Have," I corrected. "They will always be there with you. Trust me. So please, go on. Tell me. How many do you have?"

"Three. The youngest two were sick. They were so sick. I ain't never seen anything like it."

"I'm sorry."

"Me too." He uncapped the bottle and took a drink. "They lived with my ex, and she got sick. I was there, and she begged me to go to a distribution center for help. For medicine. I knew. I watched the news. Medicine wasn't helping. To me, leaving was taking a chance of being gone when I needed to be there. I kissed them though. They were sleeping, sort of in this state of unconsciousness. I told them I loved them. I knew ... I knew when I left, something inside me said I wasn't coming back. That it was the last time I'd see them."

"What happened?"

Dodge stared into the fire as he spoke. "I went to the setup place. You know, distribution. This was before the city shut down. Fighting broke out. I was there. I was detained. Tossed in the jail. No judge. No lawyer, no way to get out. Just sitting there freaking out 'cause I knew my kids were dying."

I felt his words; I felt them emotionally and physically. "I am so sorry. I am."

"Thank you."

"You said three children. What about the third?"

"My son, my oldest, is at college about eight hundred miles away. I don't know. He was probably sick too."

"You don't know. You don't. I think maybe you should go look for him? Nice to have a goal."

"I don't know. Maybe. No, I will. How can I not?" He inhaled loudly. "Looking for anyone alive right now is also a goal. Getting across a bridge. That's a goal. What about you? Kids? Husband."

I nodded. "Yeah. Two. A boy and a girl. A husband. The perfect suburban life."

"Cut short by the flu."

"No, actually. Cut short by a man drinking in his grief over the death of his own son. My family was killed instantly in a car crash months before this all went down."

"Instantly?"

I nodded. "They died on impact."

"Don't take this the wrong way, but lucky them and lucky you."

That did make me angry, and my eyes met his over the fire. "Why would you say that?"

"Because they didn't suffer. You … You didn't have to watch what this flu did to them. To hear them cry in pain, suffering, and know there was nothing you could do but wanna die right there with them." He took another drink.

There was a quiet moment. A part of me felt he was right.

Dodge broke the silence. "You said you are from Downing. How'd you end up at this end? Getting supplies?"

"No, being dead."

"I'm sorry?"

"Before this happened. I guess it was happening, but I was so stuck in my grief, I didn't know too much about the flu, nor did I care. I was out, it was after a long day of drinking, and I kept drinking. Drinking. Drinking." Almost without realizing what I was doing, I reached across for the bottle and took a drink. "A part of me just couldn't get drunk enough to numb the pain. But my body disagreed and I shut down. I fell unconscious, felt like I was having a stroke. Next thing I know, I'm in the hospital hearing about alcohol poisoning, then I hear someone say I have the flu. And then I wake up in the football stadium, wrapped in a cloth body bag right smack in the middle of all those bodies."

"Holy shit. They tossed you in with the dead?"

"Yep. I guess they thought I was dead, or didn't care. But I lost three weeks. I don't know how long I was left for dead and unconscious."

"No wonder you look so pale and weak. Babe, you gotta replenish. Take it easy. Who the hell knows how long you lay there."

"I know."

"So let me get this right." He held up his hand. "You passed out and the world was okay, you woke up and it was dead. Talk about a shocker. You thought you were dreaming?"

"Yes. I did."

"I don't know what's worse. Knowing what happened or missing it. I sat and watched the world end from inside a jail and via the news."

"That had to be hard," I said.

"It was." Dodge took another drink. Held his hands to the fire and spoke. "Every day. And every day, the men around me got sick. They eventually stopped taking them out. Then they stopped bringing food. They stopped locking us in our cells. But the news was on. It went from different newscasters every couple hours, reporting the same thing, the same death and riots. Then there was only a handful of news people, and then as the numbers dwindled in the jail and the outside world, one reporter remained. Tamika. To me she was hope that life was continuing. Then the last day she came on she looked sick. Really sick. Then she didn't come back. No one did. Hope died. The news stayed on until the power went down, but for a couple days, all we saw was the news station and an empty chair. That just about says it all, don't it? An empty chair."

"At least you knew," I said. "I've been trying to piece it together. Magazines, newspapers, the soldiers' reports. A man named Wilkes wrote them." As I reached into the suitcase for the clipboard, Dodge's hand crossed over mine and he lifted out a stack of rubber band–bound licenses.

"What are these?" he asked.

"At the military setup, they kept those. I suppose they were gonna keep track and then it got ahead of them."

He rummaged some more and found the other stacks. "You kept them all? Don't you think that's kinda sick?"

"No. Not at all." I grabbed the licenses from him. They were mine, and I felt insulted, that he was touching something personal and doing so without respect. "They are a reminder to me. I always want to remember. Those bodies out there, the ones we see everywhere, were more than corpses—they were people with names and lives and families. And these pictures, these faces, do just that. The least I can do in this screwed-up, empty world"—I held up a stack—"is acknowledge these people as more than just bodies."

Dodge closed his mouth tightly, gave a single nod and held out his hand.

"What?" I asked.

"Give me a stack."

"Why?"

"'Cause I think you got a good heart and the right idea, and I want to honor them as well. Soldiers in a battle."

I handed him a pile. "That we lost."

"Nah, we ain't lost yet. You and me are still around." He undid the rubber band and slowly lifted the first license. He stared at it—really stared, with conviction. "We ain't lost yet."

18. CHOCOLATE CANDY

It was the first time in days I didn't have a headache. I didn't wake up to daggers in my eyes or a mouth so dry my throat hurt. I did wake up to two other sensations. One was the overwhelming urge to urinate, the other was the smell of coffee.

I welcomed the aching bladder, because that meant I was hydrating. Prior to that, I'd been going nearly all day without attending to the needs of my urinary tract.

I wanted to address why I was smelling coffee so strongly, but I had to shuffle off, and when I returned, Dodge had poured me a cup. He handed me some expensive coffee shop mug filled with the piping hot brew.

"Oh my God, how did you make coffee?" I took in the warm aroma, allowing the steam to touch my nostrils, then sipped it.

"Found a coffee shop, some things people didn't take," he said. "Like a French press. Makes it easy. I love my coffee."

"Me too."

"The way you nursed that bottle last night, I'm gonna say you love your booze."

"That too."

"I'm sorry," he said. "That was wrong."

"No, it wasn't. This is good." I gestured with the mug.

"Eat up. We have a long day." He handed me a paper plate with a pancake on it. "Sorry there's no syrup. Best I can do, but that ought to buckle you down. You look much better."

"I feel better." I examined the pancake in wonder. "How are you doing this?"

"1999 Jeep Cherokee over there had camping stuff. Guess they were headed to the hills. Check it out." He pulled out a backpack. "In case we have no shelter. Small tent and a sleeping roll. I'll carry it. However, I have other plans."

"I bet you do."

"Anyhow, everything is easy when you have a fire. Pancakes are easy when you have water and a bottle of that mix." He lifted his pancake, folded it and took a bite.

"Did you go camping a lot?"

"Yeah, I did."

"How long have you been up?"

"Long enough to discover good news."

I was just about to take my first bite of the pancake, and I paused. "What's the good news?"

He produced half a smile. "We have to backtrack a mile, head down to the other expressway, but … Steel Miner Bridge is accessible."

"No, it's not, we looked down there yesterday."

"Yeah, well, it isn't collapsed; it's just a barricade, and a couple car fires. From what I could see we can get through. Have to do some small climbing, but I think once we're across the bridge we're gonna see less traffic and less remnants of pandemonium."

"Why do you say that?"

"Because the city was shut down. Not the other parts, just the city. I don't know why, because everywhere had the flu. But you lock people in, they get nuts, feel trapped, and that's what happened."

"So we'll make it across the river today?"

"Yeah, I believe so. But we'll take it slow, take it easy, and if you feel it's too much, we'll stop."

"Okay." I nodded. "But honestly, I can do this. If you weren't here, I'd have no choice, right?" I knew he agreed, and I also knew his mind was churning. I finally took a second to dive into that pancake. It was sweet and delicious. So much better than the MREs I'd been eating.

While I rested the evening before Dodge had scavenged cars, and while I slept he was thinking ahead. When I started my journey, I'd had one focus goal left, and that was to make it home. That was still my goal, but something told me Dodge had been making other plans.

I couldn't see life beyond that pancake and crossing that bridge. Dodge did.

As content as I'd been to spend my time alone before the flu, at that moment, in a desolate world, I was glad that I'd found Dodge.

<><><><>

Belly full—but not enough to bog me down—rejuvenated with some caffeine, and finally rested, I was ready to go.

At the rate we were going, we'd have to find transportation for all the things we'd gathered. Dodge had his hiker's backpack and was toting the new and improved suitcase on wheels. I had my ration bag full for both of us when needed, draped over my shoulder.

Until we got to the bridge, the conversation between us remained technical, and about our immediate plans to cross the river. Though Dodge did start to go on about the "next move" after I stopped at my house. He tossed ideas around, asking what I thought after every few.

I didn't engage much in the conversation, because I truthfully didn't know what I wanted or what I was going to do after I made it to my house. I wasn't thinking beyond that; I wasn't thinking long term. Did we honestly need to?

I liked when he talked about his son. Tyler was his name, and he was something like eight hundred miles south at a school for art. I was cautious not to say anything that might build up Dodge's hopes, because as a mother, the last thing I'd want is to start looking positively at a situation only to be crushed. And no matter how prepared one is, you are crushed by the loss of a child.

Dodge took an avoidance road with Tyler, even though the last he'd spoken to his son, the nineteen-year-old wasn't even sick. I wanted to say, "Oh, Dodge, you have to find him. You have to look." But I didn't. It had to be his decision to go, and I hoped he would.

Cars were squeezed in like sardines at the base of the bridge. A barricade was set up about twenty feet before the ramp. That, of course, was destroyed. However, what I didn't see to start with, though Dodge did upon further investigation, was that cars had plummeted to the road below. They'd piled on top of each other, and the weight of the major traffic jam on the roadside had given in, causing more vehicles to topple. This cluster of a mess had become a viable path that we could walk along.

Walk over the tops of the cars. All well and fine, but not for getting up to the bridge.

"We got this," Dodge said.

"Oh, yeah, we got this," I said sarcastically, and peered across what had become a graveyard of banged-up, piled-up cars. I had to lower myself down a slope about six feet high to the top of a black SUV, maneuver across the cars where the ramp used to be, then magically, somehow, get on the bridge. *Oh, yeah, I've got this. Right.*

Dodge left the suitcase and backpack with me, lowered himself down with ease, then reached up. "Hand me the suitcase first."

Fearful that it would knock him unconscious, I slowly lowered the bag as far as I could. I felt him grab it, and then I did the same with the backpack.

"The rations bag." He held up his hand. "Toss it down."

"You're not planning on leaving me at this point, are you?"

"What?" He laughed. "No! Would I make you coffee and pancakes? I'd have left before you woke up. Rations."

I dropped the small sack.

"Now you. Belly down so you can see where you're coming from, and trust me that I got you."

"I'd rather see where I'm going."

"Yes, well, I bet you would. But looking down, you are gonna slip. It's easier to glide feet-down to me."

"My feet will be toward you."

"I mean, with your backside up."

"I can do this. Didn't you say we got this?"

Dodge took a step backward and held out his hand. "Be my guest."

Really, how hard was it? He'd barreled down in a good couple steps—yeah, the slope was steep, but it was really only about six feet.

Six feet of concrete, to an unprepared person, was slippery. I made it halfway—three steps and I slipped. My feet went from under me, and while I made a half-assed attempt to catch myself and my pride, I still managed to tumble in a part roll, my right arm scraping against the concrete.

Dodge reached up to grab me, but it was too late. Though he did secure me and help me the rest of the way down. "You okay?"

Like a child, I peeped out a "No." I had that all too familiar stinging of a brush burn. The skin was torn, and then with a slightly delayed reaction, it started to bleed.

"That will hurt," Dodge said. He lifted the ration bag and pulled out some water. "Does it feel broke?"

Another peep. "No."

"You're bleeding." Dodge grabbed my arm.

I winced and pulled back. "Stop. Stop. That hurts."

"Oh, you stop." He uncapped the bottle with his teeth and slowly poured water over my wound. "Shake it off."

"Shake it off?"

"Shake it off. I told you not to climb down that way, didn't I? You probably got hurt a lot worse when you were a kid and fell off your bike."

"I wasn't allowed to ride a bike."

"You didn't ride a bike?"

I shook my head. "My mother wouldn't let me. She said I would get hurt."

He nodded. "I can see why she would think that."

"Dodge."

"Don't whine. Stay here. Don't move."

"Why?"

"Just … stay here."

I didn't move from my position on top of the black SUV. Dodge carried the suitcase and backpack across the cars and closer to the bridge, then returned.

"Not that I don't think you can do it, but I can't have you getting hurt."

"Are you always going to be like this?"

"No," he said. "Because *you* won't always be like this. Right now, you're still recovering. You aren't a hundred percent." He shrugged. "Maybe you are, and I'm just wrong."

"You're not wrong. I'm usually much stronger."

"Then good. I'd like to see that without you breaking a bone first." He held out his arm for me to latch on to.

I hated it. I absolutely hated the fact that he looked at me as weak. And I hated the fact that I'd fallen, that I'd looked and acted sick.

I actually debated not taking his arm and doing it myself, but I'd seen how well that had gone before.

Walking across the cars wasn't as easy as it looked. The roofs weren't strong, and twice the windows shattered just from a simple touch of my foot.

But we made it across, and Dodge, with the ration bag around his neck, climbed up to the bridge. He lay with his chest flush with the ground and extended his arm. "Hand me the suitcase first. Heaviest item out of the way."

It was heavy. Before I lifted it, I made sure the handle was all the way out, and I was only able to raise the suitcase to mid-chest. Dodge grabbed it.

I knew his request for the backpack would be next. It was on its side, and as I reached for it, I moved past the flipped-up mirror of a car. In doing so, I caught a glimpse of my reflection.

Frozen. I was absolutely frozen, staring at myself.

Was it me? I reached up to my face. I barely recognized my own reflection. No wonder Dodge looked at me the way he did. I was shocked he hadn't tried to find a wheelchair. All I could think was how Dodge had said earlier that I looked much better. If I looked "better," how bad had I looked before that? Was that even possible? My face had never been so white. I'd say it had surpassed being pale. I didn't just have dark circles *under* my eyes; they surrounded my eyes, like a raccoon. My lips? Aside from the sores, which I'd known I had, they were near colorless. With my straggly hair, even though I'd washed it back in the hotel, I looked like a walking corpse.

"Hey." Dodge whistled. "You gonna hand me that backpack?"

My head cocked in shock, I nodded and reached for the backpack, then lifted it up enough for Dodge to grab it.

A few moments later, Dodge edged his way down and pulled me over to the highest car. The edge of the bridge was still above my head.

"Alright, here's how it's going to go," he said. "Raise your arms."

I did.

"See, you're only about four inches short of touching that ledge. So I want you to step on my knee, reach up, and I'll hoist you. Get a grip, you'll have to pull a lot of your own weight, okay?"

I nodded.

"Once I see you have the ledge, I'm going to try to push you up there, so be ready. Please don't fall."

"I promise." I took a deep breath. When I stepped onto his bent leg, I could already see the ledge. I reached up and Dodge lifted me. I grabbed hold of the concrete and pulled. I was fighting and struggling to do what was essentially a glorified chin-up. Just as I was about to give up ... Well, I'd love to say I found my inner fortitude, but the truth was, Dodge gave me a good hoist.

Once my chest hit the edge, he maneuvered his hands down my legs and lifted me enough that I was able to get the rest of the way onto the bridge.

As if it would help or matter, I reached down to help Dodge. He just smiled, climbed up, then grabbed my hand.

"Good job." He shook my hand. "What's wrong?"

"Why didn't you tell me how bad I looked?"

"I told you that you didn't look well."

"It's beyond that. I saw my reflection."

"Faye."

"Yeah?"

For a moment he stared at me, then said seriously, "Now's not the time for vanity."

I couldn't help it. I actually laughed. I ... laughed. For the first time, really, it wasn't fake, it wasn't forced—it was genuine. I told him he was right, and turned. It was breathtaking, the empty bridge.

"Dodge, this looks all clear." I peered over my shoulder as he gathered our things.

"I'm betting it's that way for a while. People were trying to get out of the city, not in."

"I suppose you're right." I started to walk. "Maybe we'll get to my house in no time. Find a car and ..." A few steps down the road, I couldn't hear Dodge and I knew he wasn't walking with me. Even without a squeaky wheel, the rolling suitcase made a noise.

I stopped, turned. Dodge wasn't moving. He was staring at something in his hand.

"Dodge, what is it?"

He held out his palm. He looked shocked. "An M&M."

"Oh, don't eat that. You don't know where it's been."

"Do I look like I'm gonna eat this?"

"I don't know. Why pick it up?"

"Why is it here?" he asked.

"Someone dropped it."

"Faye, what were you eating a little bag of last night? You didn't finish."

"M&Ms. From the MRE. They were stale."

He lifted the candy to his teeth. "Dodge!" I scolded like a mother to her child.

He bit down, cringed and spit it out.

"Why would you do that? You said you weren't gonna eat it."

"I wanted to see if it was stale like those ones from last night. It was."

"Okay." I threw out my hands. "It was stale. The point?"

"The point is, if traffic ended over there, what's a piece of candy, stale nonetheless, doing over here?"

"Someone dropped it."

"Exactly."

It took me a moment and a second glance at the look on his face to see where he was going with this, what he was possibly thinking.

"Dodge, anyone could have dropped that. Before the flu. A soldier would be eating an MRE."

"But it doesn't make sense. It looks like it was just dropped."

"Do you think someone else was eating a bag of candy from an MRE and dropped it while making their way across this bridge?"

Dodge nodded. "I do. What do you think?"

"Honestly?" I paused and took a deep breath. "I believe you're thinking too hard and looking too much into it."

Dodge tossed the candy to the bridge. "You're probably right."

"I'm sorry."

"No—I am. I'm just looking for anything and everything." Almost defeated, he swung the pack over his shoulder and started walking, pulling the suitcase with him.

I didn't want to say anything else. Dodge was hopeful. He truly did believe there were other people alive. Me, I believed that if there were people out there, they'd be a lot harder to find than that tiny piece of candy on the bridge.

19. DOWNING PARK

The bridge was more than just a crossing over the river from one side of town to the next. It was a bridge to a different story.

It led to a vacant portion south of town, a section of which was barren even before the flu. Run-down businesses that had once thrived decades earlier. Pizza shops and car repair places. Not a residential area by any means. And I knew, with one glance, we'd be at my house before it was even afternoon.

Just blocks after crossing, we saw our haven. Dazzling Dan's Buy Here Pay Here Car Lot. A virtual smorgasbord for Dodge. He moved around the lot, looking in each car, almost as if searching for something in particular.

Pick one, please, I thought.

Then he did.

He broke the window to the front door of the trailer office and emerged with keys.

"Half tank of gas, I can fix this one if it breaks. I gotta plan for gas later," he said.

Later. Dodge always seemed to be thinking about later. We tossed the suitcase and backpack in the car, then after a few futile cranks, the engine turned over and we were off. We were about ten miles from my home.

I asked Dodge again if he wanted to stop at his place or his ex-wife's.

"Maybe," he replied. "Not now. I'm just not ready to see it. I know how sick they were."

"I understand."

It wasn't until a mile into our trip, as we drove through the first stretch of road with homes, that something clicked in Dodge, and I know what it was. It was the bodies on the sidewalk, the shoulder and verge of the road. Some in trash bags, some in official body bags, and others covered loosely in what looked like drapery and sheets.

Dodge turned and looked at me, then stared forward. "I think maybe I'll have to go there. I'll have to bury them. I owe them that."

"I'll help you if you want."

"I'd like that but … I'm gonna do it alone."

Another thing I understood. There were probably many reasons Dodge wanted to be alone to bury his family. The emotional aspect of it was private and personal. In a way, I was relieved he'd said he didn't want my help. Seeing a child would just be too much. I hadn't seen a body of a child at all. It horrified me to even think about it, the torment that the innocent had to endure. If I didn't see one, then maybe, in my mind, I wouldn't have to face the reality that children had suffered.

As we drove farther, I realized the river drew a clear line between the contrasts of the two areas. In the city it was panic, chaos and fear. Signs of turmoil at every corner. In the suburbs it was quiet. There were little signs that people had erupted in violence; they hadn't been caged in. They were left to die without resources. They'd brought their dead to the edge of the road like Sunday garbage.

Somehow, in my mind, I envisioned my housing plan to be unscathed, that we'd roll in and have to slow down on the speed bumps, or stop because a child's ball would roll across the street.

The strict fifteen-miles-per-hour speed limit was always adhered to. I lived in one of those housing plans that were a step shy of a gated community, where all the houses looked the same and the lawns were perfectly maintained. Where everyone pretended they had money and only a handful weren't buried beneath monstrous mortgages.

The second we pulled in, my fantasy was blown. My neighborhood was no different than any other. We'd brought out our dead just the same as the inner city.

I lowered my head. "Make the next right. That's my street."

"Doesn't look like any looting took place here."

"No," I whispered. "Everyone was too busy being sick."

I felt the car turn left and reluctantly I glanced up. "Fifth house on the right," I said. Then I looked, and a lump formed in my throat. There were bodies outside the Reeses'. The Merrimens, they'd suffered too. Mr. and Mrs. Doyle, my next door neighbors, who constantly brought me food after my family died … They were not immune. There was one body outside; I could only deduce the other was still inside, in bed, alone.

The car turned and Dodge asked, "This it?"

Looking up, I nodded.

Dodge turned off the engine. "You ready?"

Actually, I was. I needed to get inside. My house, my home, was the only thing in the world that would be normal to me. Because it was the only home on the entire street that hadn't suffered a loss to the flu.

It had battled and lost long before the sickness took the world. It was empty long before the flu claimed its victims. I opened the car door, stepped out and stared at my front door. Like open arms saying, "Come here, find comfort," my house called to me.

I was home.

20. HOME

My house had that "been away on vacation" smell. Not old and musty, just unlived in. The scent of dust and stale air, along with a hint of spoiling food from the fridge. There wasn't much in there to go bad.

Dodge brought the bags inside. I informed him I had some bottled water but not a lot. Unlike the Doyles.

"What about the Doyles?" he asked.

"Well, that Rush Spring Water truck arrived every month with bottles. You know, the big ones."

"Where do they live?"

"Next door."

"I'll be back."

"You can't go over and take their water."

Dodge paused, turned and looked at me. "Really? Are you really saying that?"

"Is it right?"

"Ask yourself what your neighbors would want you to do. Would they mind?"

I thought about it and remembered it was the Doyles. They were sweet and caring and would be the first to volunteer their water. "They'd say take it. House to the right."

Dodge left. He hadn't said much about my home. Then again, he'd only stepped in the door. The first thing I did was empty the fridge. It was odd, because I had plenty of paper products. I shopped at the bulk stores, and while Rich and the kids were alive, I went through them fast. Since their passing, one roll of paper towels no longer lasted a day; it lasted a week.

By the time I'd emptied out the refrigerator, I'd also removed some of the dust and opened the windows to air out the home. I had been lingering in the smell of death for days; I just wanted to smell something fresh. In my mind, we were going to be there a while, and when Dodge returned an hour later, I wondered if he was thinking the same thing.

He must have taken a few trips back and forth to the Doyles', because he brought in three of those big bottles. He'd also found other items—canned goods, candles, box products that were still viable.

"You looted my neighbors."

"Don't say it. They aren't using it, and it's guaranteed stock. We don't know the status of the stores yet. I plan on hitting the other houses as well. We can't live off of MREs—they're good in a pinch, but not for your digestive system."

"I'll remember that."

"Okay, these"—he pointed to the full bottles—"are for drinking and food. For cleaning, I brought some of their empty bottles. We'll use what's left in your water tank. That water can be used for washing up, and if we use it sparingly, we can get a good flush a day."

"You're thinking ahead."

"I'm looking at a woman. I'm kind of thinking a flush is a big deal." He winked.

"It is."

"You have neighbors; they have water tanks too. I just hit the Doyles' for now. I found some flashlights and candles, too."

"I see that."

"Do you mind putting the stuff somewhere? I'm … I'm going to head over to my ex's house."

"Oh, Dodge," I said, almost a whisper. "Are you sure you don't want me there?"

"No." He closed his eyes. "It's something I have to do. I'll be back."

"Good luck. I'll pray for you."

He reached for the door, paused and turned. "Lock this, please. I know things seem safe, but lock it and …" He reached behind his back and handed me a revolver. It was small, almost toy-like. "I got this from your neighbors."

I stepped back as if it were acid.

"What?" He looked confused.

"I'll lock the door, but I don't want that. I've never touched a gun, and I don't plan on starting now. I'm actually scared of them."

"Fair enough. But I'm gonna work on you getting over it."

"Dodge, seriously, if there are people left, are we really wanting to shoot them?"

"We may not have a choice. Lock the door and find a weapon, just in case. Please."

"I'll do that. Mark had a baseball bat."

"Good." He finally opened the door, glanced back at me with a nod and then left.

I stood there by the front door, peering out the wide window. Dodge got in the car. He wasn't moving with confidence like he usually did. He carried a lot of grief on his shoulders, and I felt bad for him, really bad for what he'd have to face.

He was wrong; I didn't believe bad people would break in. In fact, I didn't believe anyone was coming at all. The baseball bat would stay in the closet, but just because I'd said I would, I locked the doors.

<><><><>

Dodge was gone for a while. It even hit a point where I wondered if he was going to come back. I finished getting rid of most of the dust and then I went to the shed for the extra propane tank for the grill. I fired it up and put on a medium pot of water with a lid.

It took forever to come to a boil, even though we had a decent grill. I figured I'd make some pasta with the cans of tomatoes. Something different and filling. It was still too early in the year to hit the local farms to see what might have grown on its own. So fresh food was out, at least for the time being.

I even went to the basement, studied the water heater and found the release spout. Even though I knew no natural gas was flowing through the pipes, I still shut them down. I'd seen an earthquake movie once where that was reiterated over and over.

I cleaned up; I still looked pretty crappy, but I felt better. My own house, my own clothes. I'd have Dodge fill the buckets to take into the bathroom. The tanks on all the commodes were still filled, so our one flush per day was secure.

By the time I finished my minuscule tasks, I was pretty beat, but it was a heck of a lot easier than walking the streets. It was starting to get dark when I heard Dodge pull into the driveway. I was sitting on the back deck with my second glass of wine, and dinner was in a pot on the grill.

I felt a lump in my stomach when I heard him return, just knowing what he'd faced, what he must have gone through. Imagining that despite what he'd said, he had to have gone over there with some hope, that maybe … just maybe …

Finishing my wine, I went into the house. The door was still locked, and I opened it as he was stepping onto the porch.

For lack of anything else to say, I just said, "Hey."

He cleared his throat. He was carrying a box; I could see pictures inside it, a couple toys. And Dodge was dirty. Clearly he had been digging.

I closed the door, and couldn't help clearing my own throat. "How are you?"

Dodge just nodded.

"I left a bucket downstairs in the basement by the water heater if you want to wash up."

"I will, thanks." He placed the box on the table behind the sofa and stood there, staring at it. His hand grazed over the contents as if he wanted to grab something, but then he pulled it back.

"Dodge, if you want to talk …"

"Thank you." His head lowered and he took a deep breath. "I buried my ex-wife. It took a while—the ground wasn't as soft as I'd hoped, and to find a place in that tiny yard ... Then I made a marker."

"The ... the ..." I choked on the word. "Children?"

He shook his head. "I didn't bury them." He headed off in the direction of the basement door. "I couldn't."

"It's okay, it had to be hard ..."

"That's not it." He stopped walking. "I couldn't bury them. They weren't in the house. They weren't outside." He looked over his shoulder at me. "They just weren't there."

21. MEMORIES OVER WINE

I drank the hard stuff to forget the pain, and oddly enough, the end of the world seemed to have ended that sickening knot that would form every second I thought of my family. I no longer had to watch happy families at the store or walking down the street. No longer would I drive down the road and see a family in a van, and wish with all my heart it was me.

I hadn't had that for the last few days because everything was gone. Suddenly the world was as numb as I was, and I faded into the losses instead of standing out in my suffering.

I was in that company with Dodge.

We sat on my back deck. It was chilly, but a sweater kept me warm. We talked about our families and shared pictures. We both had daughters the exact same age, and instead of crying over their suffering we spoke of how cute they were, how grown up they wanted to be.

While the reminiscing made me smile, it did make me miss them, but I appreciated the memories I had at my home.

Dodge didn't say much about what he'd found at the house, just that the children's beds were unmade, and messy, and that they weren't there. Though when Dodge was arrested, it had still been early and the trucks were still coming by daily to collect the remains.

I wonder where they took them. Did they burn them? Or just dump them in the river. Maybe his children had been with me in that stadium.

After our meal, and before we settled on the deck with a bottle of wine, Dodge found Rich's huge road atlas in the garage along with camping equipment that he said was impressive.

That made me laugh. "Rich always wanted to camp, but he hated to get dirty. I told him we should just invest in the Doyle method."

"You must have liked the Doyles. What's the method?"

I stood from my lounge chair, walked to the railing and leaned forward. "Can't really see it clearly, but it's parked at the end of the driveway. See?"

Dodge joined me at the railing. I suppose he could see more than me. "Holy cow. That's a nice RV."

"Not RV. How did Mr. Doyle put it when we called it an RV? 'Winnebago Vista, baby.'" I shook my head. "They got it when he retired. At first his wife couldn't get him out of it. Then they took it every summer cross-country to see their daughter."

"That could come in handy." He returned to his chair and I did too.

"So what did your husband do for a living?" Dodge asked.

"A public defender."

"I'm sorry."

"That's terrible." I shook my head. "Rich could have worked at any practice, but he wanted to help those who needed it. He volunteered twice a month at a legal clinic."

"You folks are good people. Bet you were good together."

"Yes. I can say that with certainty. We were that couple that people knew would be together when they could barely walk. Old and gray. Or so we thought." I finished my wine and poured another. "Unfortunately, we'll never know."

"A lot of people will never know."

"So." I set down the map. "Why the atlas?"

"I think, Faye, we need to get you recouped and then head out."

"To where?"

"That's why I loved finding this atlas. We plot. We think. Then we go."

"Can I ask why?"

"As much as this is a great house, it won't cut it in the winter. Plus, we have to think long term. Canned goods won't last forever. We will eventually run out of bottled water. Maybe not right away, but we should plan. But I think while we are finding a place, before all that, we should do a salvation run."

I was confused, thinking he wanted to do something spiritual, like finding God somewhere in this mess. "What do you mean?"

"If you and me are alive, I'm convinced others are too. We just have to find them."

"So go on a mission to find people. Where?"

"We make a list of places, like jails and such, hospital wards, places people may be stuck. In this dead, quiet world, driving through will make a sound that will carry. If someone's alive they'll hear us."

"No one heard us today."

"That's true."

"Can I play devil's advocate?" I asked. "What about gas? Food? What about cities? Weren't they shut down? We can't effectively travel if we have to keep getting out and walking.'

"We pack supplies as if we aren't going to find stuff. We avoid major roads that would be blocked. We turn if need be. Gas is everywhere; we just have to pump it. They have reserve tanks under the stations. A generator and pump will do that."

"You've been thinking about this," I said.

"I still have a lot to work out, and we'll be here a few more days. We prepare."

"It's very ambitious."

Dodge looked at me. "Faye, we owe it to ourselves, and maybe to someone out there who needs our help, to look. If you didn't come when you did, I would have died. How many others are in that position?" He paused. "Besides, what else is there to do? Just sit around, watch the sun set and rise? Focus and mobility means survival and salvation."

I clasped my hands together and leaned forward, staring out. "Any thoughts on how we're going to get around in this salvation run?"

"How did Mr. Doyle say it?" The corner of his mouth lifted in a half-smile. "Winnebago Vista, baby."

All I could think of was my poor neighbors. They'd been generous, great people. But I bet they'd never thought they'd be the stop-and-shop convenience store in the post-apocalypse world.

22. AISLE FOURTEEN

Dodge had an answer for everything. I believed his "If I don't know it, I'll make it sound like I do" attitude was the reason he was divorced multiple times. He wasn't a bad guy, but that part of him drove me a little nuts.

He spent the whole of the next day going through my neighbors' homes, as if everything he gathered was going to fit in the Doyles' RV. It was actually named Fastball, after a band that did an old song about an elderly couple that took an RV out to die. Or something like that. The name was printed on the side.

I woke up on the second morning after falling asleep looking at the drivers' licenses and reading Wilkes' reports. Not that the reports told me anything I didn't already know, but Wilkes had gone to all that trouble and someone should look at them. His watch was secured on my wrist with an added hole I'd made so it fit.

It was May tenth. Five days since I woke up on that pile of bodies.

I definitely felt stronger, and I knew I looked better. Even Dodge finally said that I didn't look like a corpse, joking that he was fearful I was an intelligent zombie.

"Your color is back. Blood is pumping," he said. "Told you the red wine and spinach would help. Thank the Doyles."

The poor Doyles. I made a mental note to somehow pay homage to them for all the posthumous help they were giving.

It was a warm morning, and Dodge wanted to venture out to get the items he needed to create his pump. He also needed a generator and some gas cans, and of course, he found those by scouting the neighborhood. He used the gas to fill the tank of, yes, the Doyles' economy wagon. The second one we took from them.

The "Dodge plan" was to have our gas-pumping system strapped to the top of Fastball as we journeyed from small town to small town, searching out survivors and eventually a farm.

I wasn't as optimistic; it sounded kind of like a fairytale to me. And I guess at times, I projected that. I didn't understand the need for the RV; after all, it was a waste of gas. But Dodge insisted we wouldn't be able to keep stopping to find a place to stay.

<><><><><>

There was a string of super stores off Route 50—a super home store, super grocery centers and a Walmart.

They were the first true signs we saw of looting and panic shopping. Then again, the shelves weren't all that bare. At least, not of the items we needed.

The huge Home Hardware store had most of what Dodge needed to make his pump system. We took the items back to the car, and then drove across the lot to Walmart to see if they had a hose; we hadn't found one in the home store.

"Why Walmart?" I asked, thinking if they didn't have it at the home store, they wouldn't have it there.

"Cheaper." He stepped out of the car.

I rolled my eyes at his bad humor.

"Car parts, Faye. I want to find extra car parts for Fastball. Then we have them."

There he was again, always thinking ahead.

Walmart had clearly been picked through, especially the super center food section. Who would take the meat though? Even I would know better, and I was far from a survivalist. Some food items remained on the floor, knocked over, trampled on. But the things we needed were in the back. The farther back we went, the fewer things were touched.

"Grab some blankets," Dodge said, walking at a quick pace. "The good ones."

He moved ahead, leaving me behind, and I followed his orders in the blanket aisle, grabbing an armful and placing them in my cart. I looked to see if there was anything else, then decided Dodge would probably have thought of it already.

I found him in the auto section. The store was so dark, I had to rely on the huge spotlight he carried, which lit everything around him.

"Got blankets," I announced.

He turned and started to drop items into the cart.

"This stuff is not fitting in the car," I said.

"It'll fit. And I thought of other places we could stop to look for survivors. I want to put it on the atlas when we get back to the house. All part of planning our route."

"Like where?"

"Army bases."

"Army bases?"

"Yeah, and Greenbrier Mountain in West Virginia. The resort there has an old Cold War bunker. It's a casino now, but people may be hunkering down."

"I'm sure. And we're gonna open the door to the bunker and let the flu right in."

"Okay, then maybe we should hit the CDC first."

"The CDC?"

"Centers for Disease—"

"I know what it stands for—why?"

"They may be working on a cure."

"So we go to Atlanta, go to the CDC, which we probably won't get into. Get the cure and drive all the way back up to West Virginia to deliver it to the people in the bunker."

"Why do you have to be like that?" Dodge took the cart from me and started to push it.

"I'm just repeating what you said so you can hear it."

"You're being sarcastic."

"Realistic."

"How about being helpful?"

"I got the blankets, didn't I? And give me back the cart." I took hold of the handle. "You shine the light. It's spooky in here."

"And I don't mean about the blankets. I mean in general. Talk about this with me. Be a part of the plan. Have a little hope, and try not to act like it's a waste of time."

"I'm sorry, Dodge. I am. I appreciate what you're doing. My focus was only to get home. I didn't think that far ahead."

"So you didn't know what you were gonna do after you got to your house?"

"Honestly, I was probably going to die."

He stopped and faced me. "Are you serious?"

"Yeah, I am. I wanted to die before this whole mess happened. I tried, but I chickened out and messed up."

"If you really wanted to kill yourself, you would have. There's no messing up putting a gun to your head. Wait. You hate guns." He started walking again, leading the way. "You know, you had the focus to get home. Maybe you need a focus again."

"We have the plan."

"I'm thinking something to focus on. Something that you know needs you. Maybe a puppy."

"A puppy?" I laughed. "The flu killed all the dogs."

"We don't know that. We should hit a humane society or pound just to check."

"I think that's a great idea. Set them free. But I don't want a dog."

"Not a dog person, okay. A cat."

"I don't want a cat."

Dodge stopped. "What about a kid?" he said quietly.

"Oh, sure," I scoffed. "I'll just have a child in the post-flu world."

His voice dropped, and he spoke slowly, seriously. "No, I'm not kidding. What about a kid?" Dodge stood there, his flashlight shining outward, and even in the dark, he looked stunned.

"Dodge?" I went over to him.

He was facing away from me, and when I got closer, he didn't move. He just shifted his gaze to mine, then looked forward again. Was that tears forming in his eyes? Why was he suddenly so emotional?

I started to ask, but as I took another step closer to him I glanced into the beam of light, and what I saw took my breath away.

Huddled on the floor against the shelf of action hero figures at the end of aisle fourteen, eating from a bag of cheese goldfish, was a little boy. Perhaps slightly blinded by the spotlight, he stared at us with a scared and shocked expression that surely matched ours.

23. FOUND

He wanted to run. Had he not backed up into the shelf, scared out of his wits, the little boy would have taken off. No older than four or five, he was shaking. There were empty juice boxes scattered around him, and he emitted an odor that I'd smelled before—on myself. He smelled exactly like I had.

"Son," Dodge said softly.

His little eyes widened, and he whimpered in what I guessed was fear. He inched back.

"We aren't gonna hurt you." Dodge reached out his hand. "Come on. Let us help you."

The boy didn't move. I could see he'd made a little home there on the floor of the toy department. The illuminated Action Jackson Adventurer mask must have been his light source.

I moved back while Dodge cautiously went forward, not wanting to scare him away. Reaching into the cart, I grabbed one of the blankets. They were loose, bound only by a band of paper.

"What are you doing?" Dodge asked me.

"Trust me," I said, and flapped out the blanket. I didn't want to tell Dodge I thought he was failing because he was big and scary. Hell, he scared me when I first met him.

Blanket draped over my arm, I walked by Dodge and crouched a few feet from the child. I looked at him with as much motherly compassion as I could manage.

Sense it, I mentally urged. *Sense the mom in me.*

I slowly widened my arms. I stared at him, keeping my eyes on his. Wiggling my fingers slowly, I spoke as softly as I could, conveying as best as I knew how that I understood he was hurt and scared. Sometimes the simple tone of a voice can sway a child more than anything else. "Baby, come here. Come on, sweetie."

Down went the drink box and the boy jumped up, racing to me and nearly tripping over his child-like survival items. He ran straight into my arms, barreling me over and knocking me to my backside. His tiny arms wrapped around my neck so tight; he pressed his face to mine and clenched his legs to my body.

"It's okay, I have you," I whispered, cradling his head with one hand and clutching him as tightly as I could with the other. "I have you."

At that moment it didn't matter how badly he smelled, how dirty he was. He was a child, lost and scared, and he'd found safety in my embrace.

It was obvious he wasn't letting go. His arms kept tensing up, relaxing, then tensing again, as if I'd let him go if he released me.

I wouldn't. No way, no how.

Then, in the midst of that hold, what started as a whimper cascaded into a full-blown cry. The child wept uncontrollably. And then I, too, lost it and began to sob. My heart instantly broke for the little boy, for all he'd endured and experienced. The losses, the suffering. He was a child—even more so, a young one. A baby to me.

We weren't going anywhere, not yet. I emotionally couldn't move, nor did I want to. Not yet. For the time being, on the floor of that discount store, I held on to more than a broken child. I held on to the first sign of life.

24. DIRTY

Dodge gathered up a bunch of drink boxes, as many as he could find. It was something I didn't have at the house, and knowing children, getting the boy to drink water would be tough.

I think Dodge felt bad that the child hadn't responded to him, almost as if he'd wanted and needed the boy to grab on to him. That's what I thought because that's how I felt.

I needed assistance to stand, because the child wouldn't let go. In fact, he didn't let go all the way back to the house. He sat in the front seat with me, his chest to mine, his head down against me.

After the initial shock of finding him and the emotional break-down on the floor at Walmart, we were able to assess what all that small child had done. We didn't know how he'd ended up at Walmart, although there was a huge military aid station in the parking lot of the Big Bear Grocery store right across the road. Maybe he'd been there and everyone died?

We didn't know. He went to where he felt safe. Action hero fig-ures. He had crackers and drink boxes, loads of drink boxes. A mask that lit up and a bunch of dead cell phones. I could only guess he'd used them until they died, maybe as a light source or something.

How long he'd been there, we didn't know either. We didn't know anything, because the boy didn't speak.

"I don't think he ever will," Dodge said in the car.

"He'll speak again." I then aimed my voice to his ear. "You'll speak when you're ready. If you spoke before this, you'll speak after."

"The shock may have done something. We don't know what he saw."

"I can only imagine. But he still went to a safe place, found food and drinks. He was surviving on instincts. He's going to be fine. Won't you, sweetie, you'll be just fine."

His arms tensed up around my neck.

"This is unbelievable. This is the best find of the day." Dodge reached over and laid his hand on the boy's head.

The child didn't respond to the touch.

Dodge retracted his hand, rolling his fingers and making a fist while puckering his lips.

"He'll come around," I said. "You'll see."

The house wasn't far, and I hadn't even thought about what we'd do next with the child. As usual, Dodge had. When we pulled up at the house, I'd barely stepped from the car before Dodge started giving instructions.

"Fire up your grill and start heating up water. Use the stuff I took from the water heater. There are six jugs in the kitchen."

I nodded. He started walking away from the house. "Where are you going?"

"Your neighbors had a turkey fryer—I'm gonna use that for water. We can get five good gallons there too. He needs to be cleaned up, he'll feel better."

I agreed—the child did need to be bathed. He still hadn't spoken or responded. I carried him into the house and straight to the kitchen.

"I have to set you down. I want to heat up some water so you can take a bath."

He shook his head.

"I need to put you down, baby. You stay right by me, okay?"

His grip relaxed and I set him to the floor. I adjusted the blanket over his shoulders and looked at him. For the first time I saw his face in the light.

His skin was pale and he had dark circles around his eyes. His lips were dry and cracked, and there was mucus encrusted around his nose. His dirty hair was matted with something. It was so dirty I couldn't determine the color. It was going to take a while to get him clean. He stared at me with big blue eyes, looking so sad.

"Are you thirsty?"

He nodded.

"I'm gonna get the water started, and then we'll get you something more to drink. We'll eat after you get a bath."

I know that sounded trivial, and feeding the child should have been first, but he was already so germ-infested I hated the thought of him eating even another morsel.

The child stayed close to me, and when Dodge returned and fired up the turkey deep fryer, I sent him back down to a house three doors away. I knew they'd had young boys, and the child needed something to wear.

Dodge won over the boy when he returned not only with clothes, but with a couple toys as well.

"Yeah, I got him," Dodge said, so pleased with himself.

I'd known it wouldn't be long before the child stopped fearing Dodge. There was nothing to fear, and kids know—sometimes they just know.

In fact, he seemed to prefer Dodge to be the one to bathe him. I was happy about that, because Dodge really wanted to do it.

It was as if both Dodge and I were grasping on to this child, wanting any little piece of him so we could feel a little more whole ourselves.

After an hour, we had enough water to partially fill the tub. It was hot and ready, and as instructed, I started another pot.

Though I kept checking on them, I left bath time to the men. The boy didn't speak; I didn't hear his voice, but I heard Dodge talking away, making motor noises and car sounds to go with the toys he placed in the tub.

We replenished the bath repeatedly, using pretty much all the wash water we had. Dodge told me not to worry; there were plenty of homes in the housing plan.

Hours later, the bath routine was complete and the child was starving. He devoured a meal of soup, fruit snacks, two drink boxes and numerous crackers with cheese spread. I kept telling him to slow down; I didn't want him to get sick. Thankfully he didn't.

He yawned, and that, aside from crying and a whimper, was the only noise he made. Then he crawled onto the couch and fell fast asleep.

Dodge sat on one end of the couch, me on the other, watching the child by the light of the candles on the table. Neither of us could stop staring at him. His head pressed against my leg, and I ran my fingers through his pale hair. I would never have known it was blonde.

"You really got this kid clean," I said.

"It took a lot. I felt so bad for him." Dodge closed his eyes tightly. "He … He had stuff in his hair he shouldn't have had."

"Like what?"

"Like … How do I want to say this? Stringy honey."

It took a second of confusion, and then I processed what he meant. My hand shot to my mouth as I gasped.

"Flesh. Maggots …"

"How?" I asked breathily, barely able to comprehend. "How …"

"I don't know. I can guess. I think … I think they pulled a 'Faye' on him."

"What do you mean?"

"Left for dead. Piled in with the dead."

My heart thudded, and a sickening knot grabbed at my insides. I clutched my hand against the child's face. "Oh my God. This poor baby." I lost all control, and just started to cry. Even thinking about it hurt me.

"That's the only thing I can think of. He was probably with the bodies across the road, struggled out and headed to the Walmart because that was all he knew. This is just a guess, Faye, because there is no other reason for this child to have decomposing flesh on him. Thank God he wasn't in a plastic bag."

"Oh, Dodge."

"I know."

"I need a drink."

He held up a finger, stood and walked from the room. He needed one too. It was a lot to take in. I glanced down at the boy, my heart breaking. No wonder he hadn't talked.

Dodge returned with a bottle and glasses, pouring us both a measure.

"It's not a wine night," he said.

"No, it's not." I took the glass he handed me and sipped.

After a heavy sigh, Dodge sat on the couch. He carried the weight of worry along with his body. I saw it on his face, the way his shoulders slumped, how dark his eyes were.

I knew exactly what was going through his mind as he stared at the child.

It was going through mine.

For as joyous as it was to find not just another person, but a child, it was just as frightening. The thought of finding a helpless little boy was scary. If he'd been left for dead, then chances were so had another child. That was a thought I didn't want to have, but one I had to face.

25. THE FLU

Sleep did not come easily for me. I stayed on the couch, next to the boy, not wanting to be away from him at all in case he woke up.

He didn't. I checked him every time I opened my eyes. Checked to see if he was still breathing, responding to touch. Like a neurotic new mother with a newborn baby.

When I did doze off I was plagued with the dream of my awakening. Waking to darkness, restrained in that cloth wrap, struggling to get free and rolling to the bottom of the decaying pile.

If I'd been horrified, I could only imagine how the child had felt. Opening his eyes, not seeing his mother or father or anyone he knew, only lifeless bodies that looked like something he may have seen on television or in a movie.

He probably cried and screamed out, and when no one answered, he withdrew.

It didn't make sense; something was missing. If indeed he had been in a pile of bodies, how did the child get mistaken for dead?

The aroma of coffee told me Dodge was awake, and as I slipped from the couch the boy sat up.

"Hey, sweetie," I said. "You alright?"

He looked at me, the picture of innocence, and nodded.

"Thirsty? I bet you are."

Again, he nodded.

I stood. "We can get something in the kitchen."

He grabbed hold of my hand and walked with me.

Dodge was pouring coffee from the camping percolator. "Morning," he said. "Hey, little guy. You're up. How are you feeling?"

The boy didn't answer, just half-smiled.

"I'll take that as better. Look what I found next door." Dodge placed a box of Cheerios on the counter. "Unopened, should be good." He cracked open the box, then the interior bag, and grabbed a handful. "Yep." He turned to me. "Don't know a kid that doesn't like Cheerios."

"Some don't," I said.

"He does." Dodge winked. "Hey, bud. Want some?"

The boy nodded enthusiastically. After stealing a sip from my coffee, I grabbed a bowl. "Did you think of instant milk?"

"Better." He lifted a cardboard box of almond milk.

Immediately upon seeing this, the child shook his head.

"Dry it is." Dodge poured him a bowl, setting it on the kitchen table.

Instead of sitting in the seat, like he had for his dinner, the boy took the bowl and went into the other room.

"What's he doing?" I whispered, then followed.

He'd grabbed his toys from the coffee table, taken them and his bowl and sat on the floor. He was now eating in front of a blank television.

"Ah, man, that's sad. Probably waiting for his cartoon," Dodge said. "Did you ask his name yet?"

"He's not talking."

"We should call him Wally."

"Why should we—" I cringed. "Dodge, stop." I knew why he wanted that name; we'd found him at Walmart.

"If he doesn't give us a name today, he's getting Wally."

Holding my coffee, I watched the child sit, eat and play with his toys. He kept looking at the television. "Dodge, you knew about this flu. You watched the news, right?"

"That's all that was on."

"Can I ask you some questions?"

"Sure."

I slipped back into the dining room with my coffee, to be out of the boy's earshot yet still able to see him. "Tell me what you know."

"One day you're fine, the next you're dying."

"What do you mean?"

"When I was in county, the inmates would be yelling and screaming for the guards to let them out, and the next minute, you only heard moans. They went down fast, fever, symptoms … quiet."

"What were the symptoms? The magazine said flu-like."

"Yep. Fever first, stuffy nose, headache, and then the lungs start filling up. I mean, you can hear it in the chest. Every breath, thick and rumbling. You can't cough. Well, you try, but it's too thick to cough up and you struggle. You can't breathe to take a step or anything."

"You watched all those men die?" I asked.

Dodge nodded.

"I'm sorry for that."

"And I'm glad you didn't have to witness it."

"Did you … Did you hear about anyone recovering?"

"No. Why?"

"Obviously, you have some immunity …"

"See." Dodge snapped his fingers. "Yet another reason I want to go find a scientist or doctor, the CDC, something. I'm immune, I have to be. I never even got a sniffle. These questions, none of us can answer. Look at you."

"I was in a pile of bodies. I think ... I think I had it."

Dodge tilted his head. "Why do you say that?"

"When I was out of it, unconscious, I woke up a few times and heard voices. One time, they were saying I had the flu. The next thing I know, I woke up in a pile of bodies. The IV in my hand I can explain, but I can't explain why they thought I was dead. I mean ... I didn't die, obviously, and neither did he."

Dodge turned his head and looked at the child in the living room.

"Dodge, I think he had the flu. I think he beat it somehow, someway, like me. Like maybe we had some sort of minuscule immunity that allowed us to recover."

"His nose had so much dried mucus," Dodge said. "I had to soak it to get it off."

"And what killed people? Do you know?"

"The fever. But if that didn't do it, people drowned in their own mucus. See, early on, the fever didn't kill people because the hospitals were giving fever reducers. And the congestion was treated. But all that did was prolong it."

"I read about that."

"You're trying to find a connection," Dodge said.

"I am. It'll drive me nuts."

"Faye, we may never find a connection."

"Yeah, I already did. Whatever happened to me, happened to him. Something occurred, maybe we passed out, and our breathing slowed down so much that the fluid couldn't take a hold of our lungs completely. I don't know, I'm guessing here."

"Back in the old days, before they had the equipment to check for vital signs, people were mistaken for dead because their vitals slowed down so much. The flu could have kept you in a coma, and when they did a visual check of you, they just thought you were dead. Him …"

"What if it put him in a coma or some sort of deep sleep, and he beat it?"

Dodge slowly sat back in his chair. He was thinking; I saw it on his face.

"It's scary," I said, "because if they thought I was dead, and they thought he was dead, how many others fell to that as well?"

"At least one more." Dodge stood up.

"Dodge, what do you mean?"

"Think about it, Faye. I didn't at first. But I am now. The drink boxes, the phones, all those cell phones. He's like four years old. How did he know to grab a phone for light, or why grab those phones? He couldn't have carried them all."

"You think he wasn't alone?" I asked enthusiastically.

"I'm betting he wasn't."

"Where was this person?"

"Maybe getting more supplies. We never bothered to call out or look."

Dodge rushed into the living room. "Hey, bud." He crouched down by the boy. "Hey." He tapped his arm. "I have to ask you something."

The child looked at him.

"When we found you, were you by yourself?"

The boy just stared back.

"He doesn't understand, Dodge."

"Was someone with you?" Dodge pressed. "Someone who got the phones?"

After a paused, the child nodded.

I gasped at first, then looked harder at the boy. Did he really know what Dodge was saying?

"A big person. Little person?"

He nodded again.

"Big?"

The boy shook his head.

"Another kid?"

Slowly, the child nodded, and without hesitation, Dodge headed to the door.

"Dodge."

"I have to go."

"Dodge, I don't know," I said, looking at the child. He'd resumed eating and watching nothing on television. "He's confused. He's in shock. I don't think someone was with him."

"And I think it doesn't hurt to look. It does, however, stand a chance to hurt someone if we don't."

He was right. I was humbled. It didn't matter that I believed the child had spoken through confusion and just given the answer that he believed Dodge wanted to hear. We owed it to ourselves and the boy to look.

I stopped Dodge, asking him to wait. I grabbed the box of cereal and the boy.

"What are you doing, Faye?" Dodge asked.

"We're coming with you."

"Do you think it's a good idea to take him back there?"

"We won't take him in. But I do think, if we're going to search, two sets of eyes are better than one."

Whether Dodge didn't have an argument to that or he just plain didn't want to argue, I don't know. He exhaled, gave me a look and walked out.

With the boy's hand in mine, a box of cereal in the other, we followed him to the car.

More than anything, I hoped that Dodge was right, but I also believed we were chasing nothing more than a frazzled boy's word and a grown man's wish to find more people.

26. FIDDLING

The look on Dodge's face said it all. He was scared and determined. His driving was fast, and I had to ask him to slow down. We were trying to see if there was anyone else around, and speeding would inhibit that. Plus, as ridiculous as it sounded to slow down, you just never knew if someone or something might wander onto the road. Since finding the boy, we had to assume there was some likelihood that others were alive. Though I felt they may be like pollen—scattered far and wide and unable to be seen.

Dodge must have been a people person. Human contact must have played a huge part in his existence, defining him, because he seemed more focused on looking for other survivors than a way to just survive. As if finding people were some sort of validation that the world hadn't ended. Obviously it hadn't. I was there, the child was there. But Dodge needed more.

We took the same route as previously, back roads through the neighborhoods. Suddenly, the boy hit his fist against the back window.

"Dodge, slow down."

He'd heard it too, because he glanced at the rearview mirror. "What is it, bud?"

Then he spoke the first word we'd heard him say. After hitting the window once more, he looked at us both and smiled. "Home."

"Is that your street?" Dodge asked.

"Yes."

I actually exhaled with excitement. He'd spoken.

"We'll go there next. Okay?" Dodge said. "Sit back."

The boy did as he'd been told.

When Dodge began to drive again, I looked at him and whispered, "You can't take him back there. He wants to go home."

"He probably had toys and things there …"

"It'll be torture for him, Dodge. You can't take him there."

He huffed, looked in the mirror again and kept driving.

I took a moment to glance back. The child seemed happier. How easily that would shatter if we did take him to his house and no one was there. He was young, but somehow, knowing my own children at that age—and my daughter wasn't much older when she passed away—the boy had to know something. He had to have some sort of understanding. He was still in a state of fear and shock, hence why he wasn't talking. He was too old not to talk.

We hit the Walmart parking lot, and Dodge parked nearer to the back and closer to the home store. He grabbed the big flashlight and opened the door.

"Gonna run in there. I'll be back." He closed the door behind him.

I sensed tension from the boy in the back and turned in my seat. He appeared nervous. "It's okay, sweetie. Really, it is."

He didn't say anything, just undid his belt and climbed up front with me, sitting on my lap.

"Hey." I stroked his hair. "Since I got to hear that pretty voice of yours, do you know your name?"

"Yes."

"Oh, good. What is it?"

He didn't answer me. I didn't want to press; he had spoken finally, and that was already half the battle.

"Are you hungry?" I asked instead.

"No."

"How old are you?"

He held up one hand, then used his other hand to hold down his thumb.

"You're four. Wow. That's a good age."

He leaned forward in my lap and started pressing buttons. I figured it wouldn't matter. He pressed the hazard lights and they started clicking. I laughed. He inched more to the edge of my leg to play with the radio. He pushed the knob in and it lit up.

"You know the radio, don't you?"

He started to push the presets. One. Two. Three …

"Not finding anything there. No music. Want me to sing?"

He giggled.

"Oh, I got a smile and a laugh."

His tiny hand reached for the knob. He was petite; had his face not looked more mature, by his body size I would have guessed him to be about three. He wasn't skinny, just very small.

He kept fiddling with the knob, turning it and laughing at the static.

"Have news for you. That's your new music. The whole world has gone silent until we find these things called CDs. Yeah … They are round shiny things that people gave up to opt for digital. Mistake, huh?"

He continued to play.

"Bet me Dodge has a ton of CDs. No, wait, I bet he still has his grandfather's eight-tracks. He seems like the type of guy who thinks it will come back."

Static.

"Honey, let me turn that down." I reached for him as he tuned left and right.

Crackle. Static.

"On the emergency frequency"—static—"broadcasting."

Immediately, instinctively, I clutched the boy's wrist and stopped his fiddling. My heart dropped. A voice. It was a male voice, lacking emotions, steady and factual, yet real, not a computer.

A little boy in his childish curiosity had discovered what Dodge was looking for. People.

27. SOUND

"Oh my God."

"Man. It's a man," the boy said.

"I know. Shh." I turned up the radio. It wasn't a clear signal; the broadcast reminded me of when we'd take rides through the mountains and the signal would cut in and out.

"Continue. Top of the hour. Once you hit ... take ... road ..." The voice paused. "Operating on FEMA frequency, broadcasting from Ro—" A longer gap of static before the voice came back. "Again, this is Hashman. Call number alpha zulu foxtrot seven four three. Looking for survivors. Out."

Silence.

The car door swung open, and it was so sudden and unexpected, snatching my attention from the radio, that I screamed. I *really* screamed, and so did the boy.

"What the hell?" Dodge asked. "What's wrong?"

I brought my hand to my chest. "You scared us."

"How did you not see me coming out of the store?"

"We weren't watching. Dodge, he was playing with the radio."

"That's nice." Dodge lifted a bottle of water to his lips and took a drink. "I'm gonna hit the store—"

"Dodge, we heard a broadcast."

He shouldn't have taken a sip—or probably, I should have waited until he'd swallowed—because Dodge coughed in shock and splattered water on the boy. The kid giggled.

"You got a what?"

"Somebody using a radio or something," I said. "They were broadcasting. Like they were reading something."

"Was it a real voice, or maybe a programmed one?"

"Real. A man. But it was breaking up."

"If he's operating on a HAM, we may hear better at night." Dodge slid in and started playing with the radio. Turning the knob only produced silence. "What did he say?"

"Like I said, it broke up a lot. He was operating on some FEMA frequency."

"Probably tapped into the FEMA tower, or is close to one."

"He was looking for survivors. He then gave directions, but it wasn't clear."

Dodge looked over at me. "There are more people."

"At least one called Hashman, or something. He'll be back at the top of the hour."

Dodge pulled his hand from the radio. "Then we'll check back then, and keep checking back. Do you remember what station?"

"Well, you played with the knob. It was on there, but you turned the knob and I didn't look."

"Damn it." He hit the steering wheel. "Why didn't you say not to touch the knob?"

"Dodge, don't swear."

"Dodge, don't swear?" He shook his head. "Really."

"Yes, Dodge—really." I nodded down to the boy.

"Civilization ended, in case you didn't get the memo."

"No, it didn't end." I covered the child's ears. "Just because everyone died, it doesn't mean we have to lose all—"

He cut me off. "Faye. Please."

I gasped. "What is wrong with you?"

"I'm … I'm sorry. I'm frustrated, and I'm going back in there."

"What did you find?"

"No one was there. But the crackers were gone."

"Dodge? The crackers were gone? What do you mean?"

"Exactly what I said. The crackers were gone. The ones he was eating, the package was gone."

"Are you sure?"

Dodge looked at me slowly, and when he spoke he sounded eerily calm. "Why do you do that?"

"I think you're looking."

"Damn it."

"Dodge."

"Someone was there." He slid back out of the car. "And why aren't they coming out?"

"You're taking the word of a child."

"I didn't see the crackers."

"Maybe we kicked them."

"And *maybe* someone took them." Surprising me, he reached in and honked the horn.

I cringed. "Dodge."

"Loud." The boy covered his ears.

"Just ignore him." Dodge blasted the horn again for a few seconds.

"Dodge, stop."

He ignored me. He hollered across the empty parking lot, his voice sounding bigger than he was. "Anyone here? I know you are here!"

The boy cowered against me.

"Dodge!"

Again he reached in and beeped for three seconds, then yelled, "Hello! Is anyone here! Anyone alive!" Another beep.

"Dodge!"

I was ignored. I urged the boy to get back in the back seat and cover his ears. Dodge was obviously frustrated and felt as if he were failing, but what he was really failing at was seeing how frightened he was making the child.

"Dodge, you're scaring the boy."

"Faye, I know someone is here." He honked again, then yelled.

I had to wonder if Dodge was having a mental breakdown. If I couldn't get him to stop yelling, the least I could do was get him to stop honking the horn and scaring the child. I stepped from the car, walked around and slammed his door before he could reach in again.

"Anyone out here!" he cried out.

"Dodge. Please."

"Faye, I know it. I feel it." He faced me. "Someone is here."

"Okay, I believe you, but please stop scaring—"

"You took him!" The voice echoed, bouncing against the buildings. It was hard to pinpoint a direction. I did know one thing—whoever was shouting was young and male.

We both stopped.

"You took him from me! You took my brother!"

Dodge and I simultaneously turned to look toward the home store building.

"You took my brother!"

A small figure was running full speed our way from across the home store lot.

"I want my brother. You took my brother. You took him!" the young boy screamed. He was tall, thin, maybe nine years old. "You took my brother!" And then, fifteen feet from where we stood, he stopped and dropped to his knees. His head lowered, his arms at his sides, he looked as if he'd just emotionally drowned in that moment. "You took my brother," he said, sobbing, "but you didn't take me." His sadness carried to us in waves as his shoulders heaved. "You didn't take me."

28. SEPARATED

For as much as Dodge and I seemed to be a mismatch, one thing we had in common was the gut instinct to be a parent. That little boy sobbing in the middle of a barren parking lot was a magnet pulling at me.

Once I was able to take it in, breathe and move, I took a step toward him, and Dodge moved at the same time. But the front door of the car opened, and before we could reach the child sitting on the ground, the younger boy blasted between me and Dodge and ran to him.

It was a powerful moment. So much so that I heard an emotional groan coming from Dodge.

The boys wrapped their arms so hard around each other, their embrace so tight, that they rolled to the pavement.

They were indeed brothers. Only brothers would be like that.

The older boy was crying with joy. "Darie," he said. "I thought they stole you from me. I thought I'd never see you again." The embrace was more than gratitude; it was a need, and it was a bond. As much as air, food and water, that child needed his little brother.

Dodge lowered his head and brought his fingers to the corners of his eyes.

I was beyond humbled. Dodge had been right; his gut instinct had been absolutely right. He'd known it and felt it, and I hadn't. I went over to him and waited until I had his attention. "I'm sorry."

"Why are you apologizing?"

"Because I doubted you again."

"It's alright, really. More than anything," he said, sniffling, "I'm glad you were wrong."

I looked at the brothers, still embracing and joyful. "Me too."

<><><><>

I knew the second the reunion calmed down that we weren't leaving that lot. Not yet.

Both boys walked to us, holding hands, and before I could say it, Dodge did. "I'm sorry," he said to the older child. "I really am. If we'd known you were here, we would have found you. Are you okay?"

"I am now that I have my brother," he replied. "He's all clean and don't smell."

Dodge smiled.

The boy wasn't from the area. It was evident in his dialect, his southern way of speaking. He really wasn't older than nine. Maybe even eight. His face was young, but unlike the younger child, whom he'd called Darie, he wasn't dirty or pale.

"What's your name?" I asked.

"George," he said. "My brother is Darren. We call him Darie."

I reached out to him. "Well, I am—"

"Faye," said Darie, and then he pointed to Dodge. "Dodd."

"Well, I'm …" Dodge paused. "Dodd works. George?"

"Yes."

"Kind of a grown-up name."

"You ain't gonna make fun of my name like the kids in school, are you? You look like a bully, and you took my brother."

Dodge huffed. "I'm not a bully. And your brother was alone and scared."

"I was going to get more food and water. I came back. You were getting in the car," George said. "I chased you, I screamed for you to stop, but you kept on driving. You kept on going."

Dodge closed his eyes and lowered his head. "I'm sorry. That had to be really scary."

"I ran after you. But I lost you. I only came back 'cause I thought Darie would tell you about me."

I crouched down to be at George's level. "He hasn't spoken, but Dodge came back because he realized that your brother wasn't alone."

"I wouldn't leave my brother, I searched too hard for him."

"And I would have never, ever left you," Dodge said. "I swear. Is there anyone else around here? Anyone?"

George shook his head. "No, I looked."

"Your brother pointed to a street," Dodge said. "Said it was home."

George leaned away from Darie. "We can't go there. No one's there."

I stood. "And no one is around here?"

"Listen, guy." Dodge laid his hand on George's shoulder. "I know you've been a great big brother and taken care of Darie. But you know what—can you let us take care of you? We'd feel a lot better if you came with us."

"You got food?" he asked.

"Yes, we do," Dodge replied.

"Anything hot?"

Darie answered that one. "Soup."

"Well then, come on, Darie." George grabbed his little brother's hand and opened the back door of the car. "Since they fed you soup and gave you a bath, got all that gross stuff off of you, they can't be all that bad."

Dodge waited until the brothers were inside, then closed the car door. "We aren't that bad."

"No, we're not."

"Yet, you just got another focus, Faye. A pretty good one, I'd say."

"Yeah, I did." I walked around to my side of the car and got inside. George was buckling in next to his brother. I was anxious to get them back to my house, to get George fed and hear what he had to say. He'd mentioned he'd searched hard for Darie. What did that mean? George was another side of the story, a different side. I was full of questions, but I didn't want to ask until he showed signs that he wanted to talk.

Right then, he was enjoying his brother.

The second trip to Walmart had been an eventful one, full of surprises, all good. Not only did we hear the radio, we found another survivor, another child.

In a world so dark and dismal, reeking of death, we'd been able to find a good, solid aroma of hope.

29. FAMILY

George gobbled his soup, and I could see in Dodge's face that he was waiting to pounce on the boy with questions. The only things he had volunteered was that he and his family had only just moved to the area from Georgia, and he was really hungry.

Darie was so cute, just watching his brother with pride. He barely touched his lunch, he was so excited. I had to keep reminding him to eat.

"Oh, yeah, fruit snacks." After slurping the last of his broth, George grabbed the pack.

Down came Dodge's hand, stopping him. "Talk first."

"Oh my God, Dodge," I said vehemently. "He's not our prisoner."

George's mouth puckered. "Why do you pick on me?"

"I'm not picking on you," Dodge said defensively.

"Then you don't like me."

"Why would you say that?"

"You left me behind."

"She left you too." Dodge pointed at me.

I gasped. "I wasn't driving."

"She wasn't driving."

After a grumble, Dodge handed the snacks back to George. "How old are you?"

"Nine and a half."

Eyebrow cocked, Dodge leaned toward him, examining him. "You sure you aren't a forty-year-old man in there? You have the name for it."

"Quit picking on me."

"You're picking on him," I said.

"I am not. He doesn't talk like a kid and he has a grown-up name."

"That's because my mom and dad didn't want us boys having weird names. They wanted our names grown up, for when we get old like you," he said to Dodge.

I smiled.

"Mommy." Darie lowered his head.

"Now see, you made him cry." George scooted closer to his brother. "Mommy had to go away to that place I told you about. We're special because we get to start a new world."

I laid my hand on George's back. "I'm very sorry about your mom."

"And Dad," George said, now picking at his snacks instead of gobbling them. "I know I said no one is home, but I'd like to go back there and get pictures. Darie's so young; I want him to remember how pretty our mom was."

"Maybe even get a few of your things?" I suggested.

"What happened?" Dodge asked. "Can you tell us?"

George shifted his eyes from me to Dodge. "You don't know what happened?"

"I do," Dodge said. "Sort of. I was getting supplies, some medicine, and a riot broke out. You know what that is, right, a big fight. I wasn't fighting, but the police grabbed me and put me in jail with a lot of other people. I never saw how things ended."

"What about you?" George asked me.

"It's scary, what happened to me. I was in the hospital when the flu started. I heard them say I'd caught it. But I got confused, see, because I woke up in a big pile of—" I cleared my throat. "Garbage."

"Bodies," George said. "You mean bodies. I can take it. I know. So, you too?"

I shook my head. "Me too? Is that where you were?"

"No. I never got sick. But Darie was tossed out. I found him though, I found my brother. 'Cause I knew. I knew."

"How?" Dodge asked. "We just want to know how you boys survived. What happened in this area?"

George sipped his water, then reached across the table for a toy truck and handed it to Darie to occupy him. "My dad got sick first. Real sick. Like he came home from work, and I heard my mom say he was fevered."

Dodge asked, "Do you know if this was before or after they shut down the city?"

"I think it was before, because my dad worked in this city. I don't know. I do know it was on the news all the time and that they closed the schools."

I turned to Dodge. "Do you remember when they closed the schools?"

"Yeah, that was about the time I got arrested."

"My mom wouldn't let us near our dad," George said. "She shut him in the room and said for us to keep away. He was sick. Darie didn't understand, but I did. The day my dad died was the day before they closed the city, because I remember my mom crying. The next day she got sick and so did Darie. I don't know how she knew, but they opened a help place by the Walmart."

"Near where we found you?" I asked.

George nodded. "We all went. She could barely drive, she was so sick. We had to leave the car and walk. She was more sick than Darie, but he was crying. We got there, and there were so many people, but my mom and Darie both got seen by some doctor. I stayed with them. They had them in different tents though. They made me help."

"What do you mean, made you help?" Dodge said.

"I wasn't sick, so I had to get water for the sick people, carry blankets and run messages. I didn't want to leave my mom, but they made me."

"Oh, honey." I placed my hand on his cheek. "I am so sorry you had to see all that."

"Everyone was dying. It seemed like every time I turned around they were taking out more bodies and bringing more in. When my mom died, I just sat with Darie. He wasn't good; he was in that deep sleep. All the sick people got in this deep sleep. Some moaned, some didn't."

I asked, "How did Darie end up being put with other dead people?"

"I shouldn't have left him. I shouldn't have. They asked me to run and tell the major guy that they had more bodies, but I couldn't find the major. I couldn't. I looked. I think he died or was sick. When I got back, they had taken Darie out, and said he was dead. I told them he wasn't, he just looked it, but they didn't listen."

He paused to take another drink. "I ran off, and I cried. I didn't know what to do. Where do I go? I didn't even see that many people walking around anymore. It was scary. And then I saw it. I was sitting in the parking lot and I saw someone shake in a body bag. They were struggling, fighting to get free. A soldier went over and opened the body bag, and the man sat up and the soldier shot him."

I gasped, loudly, but George was still talking. "I thought it was a zombie," he said. "Even the soldier said it. That night they shot another. They all said it. Zombies. It scared me, and so I decided to run home, and that's when I saw another person get up from a pile. I started to scream. He was old. Older than you guys. He reached out his hand and said, 'Help me.'"

"That's when you knew he wasn't dead?" Dodge asked.

George nodded. "Yep. I watch movies. Never saw a zombie talk, so I ran back to the help place. There were only a couple soldiers left, and I told them about the man. They went to him, but I heard a shot. I think they shot him, too. I slept in the Walmart, and the next morning, no one was around. At least walking. That's when it hit me. What if Darie wasn't dead? I didn't think he was—I told them that. So I just started calling out his name over and over."

Darie peered up from his toy. "He saved me. I was stuck. I called him."

"And I heard him," George said. "Boy, was I happy. But I ran with Darie and hid him in the back of that Walmart. I didn't want anyone to shoot him."

Dodge spoke up. "Did you see anyone else get up after Darie?"

George shook his head. "I didn't see anyone get up, but I did see a teenager. He walked off in another direction, said he had to find his mom."

Dodge's hand went to his mouth, slid down to his jaw. "They shot people. They thought it was *The Walking Dead*. Ridiculous."

"I did too," I said. "When I woke up."

"Me too," George added. "There could be more people. Like Darie, they only looked dead."

"He's right," I said. "There could be more. Your gut instinct to find survivors may be right on."

"You know and I know, if they were in a plastic bag, they suffocated," Dodge said sadly.

"They ran out," George said quickly. "At least, where I was. They were putting kids and small people in sheets, and saving the bags for bigger people."

"Must have been everywhere," I said. "I wasn't in a bag. Of course, I'm probably considered small now. I wasn't before the kids died."

George looked at me. "I'm sorry."

"Thank you." I touched his arm. "They died before all this, in an accident."

George turned to Dodge. "How about you? Did you have kids?"

Dodge nodded. "Yeah, I did. They were sick. That's who I was getting medication for."

"Did you see them die?" George asked.

"I was in jail."

"Then you have to go check," George said. "They may wake up. You have to find where they put them. They may not have had that other thing."

"What other thing?" I asked.

"The blood. My mom had it, but Darie didn't. That's how I knew. All the people I saw that died were bleeding from their ears and nose, but Darie didn't. The teenager didn't have blood and neither did the old man."

"I didn't," I said. All of a sudden, it hit me. Dodge went to his house to bury his kids, and they weren't there. Filled with excitement, I turned to Dodge to suggest that maybe his kids had woken from a coma—but I didn't. I stopped. Even putting that notion in his mind was cruel. The last thing I wanted to do was send Dodge on a chase for heartache.

"Did they have it?" George asked Dodge. "Did you see the blood?"

"I … They were gone."

George inhaled loudly. "Oh, then you have to go look. You have to. You have to just check like I did. If they woke up they're scared."

"Dodge," I whispered. In my heart and in my mind, I felt he needed to go. It was his choice, though.

"I'll go with you if you want. I can help you think like a kid, think of places they went. And I can yell real loud like I did for Darie."

Dodge laid his hand on top of George's head. "I'd like that. Let's head out while it's still daylight."

I watched George explain to Darie that he'd be back, then he kissed his brother before he and Dodge left.

Dodge wasn't enthused; I guess it was a defense mechanism, saving himself from the possibility of being crushed again. I could tell he wasn't holding high hopes that his kids were alive, but he wasn't giving up either.

I expected no less from Dodge.

30. ROMERO

It was the hardest part of George's story to swallow, yet the easiest, for some reason, to rationalize. It made sense in a sick, demented way.

For decades, modern movie-making had portrayed them as monsters that could exist. A world that could turn on a dime. No one really saw them for what they were. I'd always believed, as scary as they were, they were actually a metaphor for the human race. The walking dead, the undead, zombies.

Mere shells of human beings, moving on instinct. Killing without thought, striving to keep going even though there was no reason to at the time. Impossible to stop.

The industry recycled the brainchild of a genius independent filmmaker, and society eventually thrived on it. It was at one time such an infatuation that people literally planned for an apocalypse of the undead. They waited for a world besieged by a mystery illness, only to have it produce beings that rose from the dead.

And here it was. It had happened, only those who rose were never really dead to begin with. They were killed instantly. Handed a chance at life, only to have it taken away either by suffocation in a plastic body bag or a bullet in their head. Mistaken for dead, all because of a pop culture phenomenon that had told us it was possible that decaying flesh, a non-living organism without blood, circulation, heartbeat or breath, could stand up and devour another being.

It was sad. What a pathetic situation, and I'd fallen into the trap as well. How many times did I stop, look over my shoulder and wait for the carnivorous creatures to get me?

They never did.

How many would have lived?

Would I have truly awoken to a dead world, had someone taken the time to see what an eight-year-old boy saw? Something so minor, yet obvious. If a child saw the difference between the onset of one illness and another, then why didn't the experts?

They didn't care. It was the big one, and they were overrun.

Though I hardly believe it was fifty-fifty. I distinctively remember seeing blood on both Wilkes and Stevens. Since it hadn't been a whole slew of people sitting up at once, maybe it was ten percent. Still, ten percent who'd recovered along with those like Dodge and George was a hell of a lot more people than were around right now.

It was a dead, empty world. No matter how many people were out there.

I heard them because the world was so dead. We were sitting on the deck, Darie at my feet, building with tiny blocks. The car horn beeped. Darie looked up. Like me, maybe he was hoping it was other people. Then we heard Dodge's big booming voice, along with George's.

"Brad! Lucy! Brad! Lucy! Are you there?"

"Brad!"

"Lucy!"

Honk. Honk.

I don't know how far from us they were, but they sounded distant, and they faded, moving on, searching farther away.

But they were searching. Listening to them call out with passion and desperation, I prayed that I'd hear a single child's voice respond. Maybe someone calling out, "Daddy."

I didn't. I just heard them shouting, and then they moved on.

If diligence for their efforts garnished a reward, then a hundred children would run out and answer their call. In a quiet world, the smallest of sounds travels, and so does silence.

That was their response.

Silence.

The weather was warm and the stench of bodies hadn't arrived, so I stayed on the deck for a while with Darie. Listening for life, and hoping a resolution would come for Dodge. Because without ever seeing his children's bodies, Dodge really would never know.

31. RADIO SHACK

They were gone for hours. Darie even took a nap. I'd forgotten how boring it could be when there was nothing to do. I tried to show the boy a card game, but he didn't grasp it.

About four hours after they left, I heard them pull into the driveway. Visions of a happy Dodge accompanied by his children were shattered when I saw them get out of the car.

Dodge was hard to read, but George didn't look happy; he actually looked worse than Dodge. As if he'd lost the big game.

I held the door open for them and George walked in first.

"We looked everywhere, Miss Faye. Everywhere. Called out real loud. My throat is sore."

"Dodge?" I looked at him.

He did that closed-mouth smile thing, but it was a sad smile.

"We checked the police station, the toy store," George said. "Their friends' houses. School. We'll go again, but Dodge said it was getting dark so we had to come back."

"I left some water on the sink in the powder room," I said. "Why don't you take Darie and wash up? We'll make dinner."

"Okay." George sought out his brother. "Let's go, Darie."

"Don't flush," I called as the boys darted out.

"That kid," Dodge said, "has got to be the most determined human being I have ever met in my life. If I had one half his determination, I would have been a doctor."

"Did you want to be?" I asked, closing the door.

"Faye, do I look like a doctor? I was just saying. I mean, every corner, he had a new idea. So I just went with it."

"Maybe he has a gut feeling. You get those."

"Yeah, I do. We'll go out again tomorrow. Call out."

"So you think your kids are out there?"

Dodge slowly lifted his eyes and looked at me. "No," he said sadly.

"How do you know?"

He lowered his voice. "He didn't go in the house with me. I did. I didn't have the heart to tell him. He was so excited about meeting my kids. Asked about them, but … I didn't think about it when I went before. There was blood. Not a lot, but blood on the kids' pillow cases."

"Oh, Dodge, I'm so sorry." I reached for him.

"No, it's okay." He grabbed my hand. "I've been coming to terms with it since long before I went looking."

"So why go back out?"

"Same reason we went back to Walmart. Just in case. Even if it isn't my kids, it could be someone else's. Or anyone. That teenager is out there, right?"

"If he didn't get shot."

"That too. But we gotta look. The ones like you and Darie that were wrapped in a cloth, they'll wake up. If there are any survivors, we have to exhaust every corner before we turn the next. There are others out there. And that voice you heard on the radio confirms it. We just have to find out where."

<><><><>

The boys picked at their dinner. I blamed that on Dodge, for finding a bag of chocolate Kisses and allowing the boys to devour it. But it had another effect; they were on such a sugar high, they raced around the house carefree until they both crashed.

It was good to see them running and laughing. Children are resilient, and that gave me hope.

Dodge told me that while he and George were out, they'd stopped at a Radio Shack and grabbed parts for a transceiver and receiver. Dodge's first priority was to pick up that radio signal. Then he'd get the CB or whatever it was he'd picked up to work, and make calls out. He hadn't had any luck using the car radio.

The man said he'd call out every hour. But it was like a needle in a haystack—until I suggested that we try dumb luck again.

Just before bedtime, we put Darie in front of the receiver, allowing him to play with the knobs. It worked like a charm. Sure enough, the child tuned into the man AZF743.

We cheered and congratulated him. Darie was proud, though I don't think he quite understood what he'd done.

It was the end of the broadcast, but we'd found the station.

The boys passed out on a makeshift bed in the living room, while Dodge and me, being our typical evening alcoholics, waited by the receiver on the deck.

"I once heard," Dodge said, "that signals are better at night. Bounce off the moon, or something."

"What if he doesn't make calls at night? He has to reserve battery power."

"Yeah, he does. There'll be a point where he'll stop for the night. I just … I just want to hear where he's calling from."

"Who do you think he is?" I asked. "Doctor? Government?"

"Probably just some guy out there, looking for people. And that kind of worries me."

"Why is that?"

Dodge took a drink of his wine. "People lived, Faye. Just because the world died, didn't mean all the bad did too. Calling out is inviting the bad."

"We can't think that way, Dodge. We can't."

"It's a truth we have to face. Those who aren't resourceful may get violent. We're resourceful. We have to watch."

"No, you ..." I sipped some wine. "*You* are resourceful. Me, I tag along."

"You do better than you think. I do want to teach you to shoot."

"No. No." I shook my head. "I don't touch guns."

"Faye, you need to learn," he said. "Why are you so scared of them?"

"I hate them. My father was a huge gun person. He was shot and killed when I was nine, by his friend. It was an accident, but still."

"I'm sorry. I didn't know that."

"I didn't tell you." I peered down at my Wilkes watch. "It's almost time."

"You changed the subject."

"I hate guns."

"Will you think about it?" Dodge asked. "You don't know. What if we're traveling …"

"Why are we traveling now? We have the boys."

"We can't stay here. Winter will be tough, and we have to think long term. We have those boys now. We have to look for others, for this AZF743. And you have to learn to shoot. If something should happen to me, you have to protect these kids."

"Dodge, nothing is gonna happen to you." As soon as I'd said that, I realized I was always countering Dodge. Going against everything he said. He wanted to look for survivors, I said there weren't any. I exhaled. "I'll think about it."

"Thank you."

Just as we exchanged a look, a single tone, short and sweet, rang out over the speaker. I don't know if it was the moon, the night or the receiver that Dodge had hooked up to the radio—whatever it was, there was no static, no interference. Just a clean, crisp radio signal.

We weren't the only pocket of civilization remaining.

We both dove from our chairs to the decking and scooted to the radio, as if we couldn't hear sitting a few feet away. I clutched Dodge's

192

hand with excitement and waited with bated breath to hear what was going to be said.

One thing was for certain. Others were indeed alive out there. Even if it was only one man who called himself Hashman AZF743, he was alive and well and broadcasting from somewhere in the wonderful state of Kentucky.

32. LISTEN

"This is Hashman. Call number alpha zulu foxtrot seven four three. Looking for survivors. Located Interstate Seventy, one mile west of Central City, Kentucky. There will be a convoy moving out from Wendell H. Ford Regional Training Center. On the one-month mark of the fall, May twentieth, at zero eight hundred, the convoy will leave for an undisclosed farming location in the panhandle." The man, who spoke as if he were reading, paused. When he started again, he'd taken on a different tone. "Life is out there. I see it. I'm gonna keep calling out. We need hands. We need survivors. This is the last call of the night. Will resume at zero six hundred hours. This is Hashman. Call number alpha zulu foxtrot seven four three. Looking for survivors. Out."

That was it.

The radio went silent, as if it weren't even switched on.

"Will he say anything different tomorrow?" I asked.

Dodge shook his head and stood up with a groan. "I don't know." He grabbed his wine and downed it. "What do you suppose he meant?"

"What part?"

"'We need hands.'"

"Don't you think that's obvious?" I said. "They're headed to a farming area. They need people to help farm. But why, Dodge, wouldn't the base call out?"

"Honestly, I have heard it said in situations like catastrophes, the HAM operator is the first line of civil defense. This guy probably has the antenna which bounces it off the ionosphere. Most radios aren't cutting through thousands of miles."

"We're not thousands of miles from there."

"Nope, only about six hundred."

"You brought those other radios, Dodge. You may be able to make contact."

"I'm gonna try. I'm also going to hope this guy gives more information." Dodge poured another glass of wine and sat down. "Why the base? Is there still a government left?"

"Maybe there is, down south."

Dodge shrugged. "Hard to say. I mean, this guy sounded desperate. That one moment, he paused and sounded ... sincere and desperate."

"So why set a date?" I joined him, sitting down as well. "I mean, really, if you need that many people, why set a convoy date? Why a convoy? Why not just give directions to the farm?"

"Lots of reasons for that, Faye. One, there is safety in numbers, and two, not everyone that survived is good. Things will eventually get desperate."

I didn't believe that. I mean, I could see it ten years from now, but not at the moment, not in the mourning stage. "Not yet, Dodge. The world is still grief stricken, struggling and lost."

"Faye." He almost laughed my name, as if ridiculing me. "You think the bad guys are gonna stop to grieve?"

"Really?"

"I'm sorry."

"Really. You're so certain the bad guys all survived."

"Don't." Dodge held up a finger. "I didn't say that. I'm just saying, bad survived. Bad will be bad."

"And what is the basis for this? Movies? Books?"

"Man has proven time and time again, that when faced with desperate situations they do desperate things."

"And man has proven time and time again, that when faced with extraordinary circumstances, he rises to the occasion."

"Please, Faye, don't tell me you are that naive."

"No, I'm not. I just believe ... Not yet. Not yet. It won't happen yet."

"People loot."

"We loot." I looked at him. "We have looted. What makes us so different? Because we're not out of control, like the riots on the news? Those riots, those people in the magazines were just fighting for a piece of what was left. Dodge, there is nothing left but a handful of people. There *is* no precedence here."

"There is precedence. Maybe not for the end of the world, but there is precedence."

"How do we know this isn't beyond us?"

Dodge nearly choked on his wine. "Like a spiritual thing?"

"Yes, how do we know?"

"What ... And I'm not making fun of you, but why would you say that?"

"It's just odd, don't you think, that we find two innocent children, and in a jail that holds three thousand criminals, I just so happen to stumble upon the one immune man who is a good guy? How do we know? Maybe only the good survived."

Dodge smiled. "That's cute."

He downed yet another glass of wine, which prompted me to catch up. A refill of both our glasses, and I was glad I was an alcoholic and had plenty in stock.

"God did it once before, you know," I said. "I mean, with Noah. A boat and a handful of people and animals. All good. But you know, I did hear Noah was a drunk."

Dodge looked down to his drink. "Maybe history does repeat." He raised his glass. "Here's to Noah."

We clinked glasses. "Here's to you believing there was still life out there."

"And you didn't?" he asked.

What I wanted to say was, "I really didn't care if there was," but I didn't say that. I just gave a half-smile and finished our toast with a sip of wine.

33. BACK STORY

I had spent five nights with Dodge, ending each evening talking and consuming some sort of alcohol, but in those five nights, I learned very little about who he was.

He didn't finish high school. He was from a single-parent family, and he quit school to get a job so he could help his mother with the bills. He had a younger brother who died in combat. Dodge had always worked on cars.

He lived a simple life. He was married at twenty, divorced at twenty-four, and he had one son to that marriage—that was Tyler. His other two children, Brad and Lucy, were to his second wife. That marriage only lasted four years.

It was funny, because he teased me that I'd actually had the perfect sitcom, suburban life.

In actuality, I did. Up until the accident. Who actually thinks it might happen? I certainly didn't. I just know my life ended that day, and everything else was minor. Even the world coming to a grinding halt.

Dodge was strong, determined, and his infatuation with cars probably played a huge role in his instinct to find a solution and fix it all. He pre-planned everything, down to each minor detail.

I had a feeling George was a lot like Dodge. That child got up right after him, filled with enthusiasm for the day. Darie not so much; he had found his way to me during the night, cuddled against me, and was still asleep when a bubbly and upbeat George entered the room.

Of course, George and his enthusiasm woke up Darie. He reminded me of my son, Mark, whenever he'd had something he wanted to do. Up early, raring to go. George was ready to go with Dodge to look for survivors.

"Are we gonna go look today, Dodge?" he asked. "Are we?"

"Yeah, we're gonna go."

"I hope we find people. I do. I bet it's a good feeling," George said. "I know when I found Darie it was a great feeling. Then again, it was my brother, and it wouldn't be nice if I didn't feel great about it."

"We'll look for people," Dodge said. "But before we do, I need to finish putting together my pump."

Dodge's pump, that was right. With all that had happened, I'd forgotten about his plan for the pump. His means to get gasoline out of any reserve tank at any station. It would work in theory—strap the system to the top of Fastball, the RV, and use it to get the gas.

Dodge planned on testing that theory today. He also stated he wanted to get more maps. He told the boys about the radio call, telling the story with such hope. Dodge made it a point to explain it was May twelfth and we had only five days until we could leave, because there had to be an allotted time in case they ran into trouble.

The kids showed Christmas excitement over everything Dodge said. He actually got George all geared up to watch him build the pump. He took both boys out to the driveway. He was a natural with them.

I watched them from the window, Dodge lifting tools, showing each one to the boys. Teaching them.

Dodge was grieving—how could he not be? However, somehow in the middle of his grief, he was focused on those boys.

He'd told me once, before we found Darie, that I needed a focus. I needed something or someone to need me. Dodge had found that. He'd found it in the boys, and now they were his purpose for forging ahead. I'd love to say I was envious, but I couldn't. Reeling in the shock of all that was happening and all that had happened to me, I wasn't quite sure I wanted to find a purpose. Because any purpose I'd had in this life was long gone before the flu even started.

34. CONTACT

Who knew that May twelfth was going to be such a pivotal day?

Dodge and the boys finished the pump, and they were one hundred percent certain it was going to work. They couldn't wait to try it out when they went out looking for people.

It was nearing lunch time and none of them had eaten, so not only did I make them lunch, I packed them a snack.

I really didn't want Dodge to take Darie with him to test out something that could blow up.

"Oh, it's fine, get in the car," Dodge said.

"Really, I'm not going."

"You sick?"

"No, I just don't want to ride around the city. I want to stay home."

"And do what?"

"Why do I have to do anything?"

"Faye, we only have a couple days until we leave," Dodge said. "Well, while you're sitting around, you may as well play with the radio."

"You mean listen for hash guy?"

"No, the other one. Start calling out. Each channel, call out, wait, call out again, and give it a minute then try another channel."

"Dodge, really?"

"I hate when you say that word. You say it all the time. Quit."

"Quit?" I threw up my hands.

"Come with us, Faye. The boys want to search."

"Take them searching. I'm fine."

"You're missing out."

Missing out? Did he really say that? I rolled my eyes.

I locked the door after he and the boys left, at his request. They got in the car like they were heading to a baseball game. It was weird.

The house was quiet. It sounded quiet and felt it, too. As I started to clean up from lunch, I saw Dodge had left the main atlas on the table. He had two routes marked to Kentucky, highlighted with different color markers.

I was sure it wouldn't be long before he started packing up Fastball. Dodge was thinking ahead on everything. I still didn't understand the need to go south and join the group of people, if indeed there was a group of people. For all we knew it could have been one man in a house on Interstate 70 hoping for someone to come and join him in a pipe dream to find a farm in the panhandle. Were there even farms down there?

I know if I told Dodge that, he'd say it was one more person.

The radio was next to Dodge's map. I lifted it, turned it on; it seemed easy enough.

Volume. Channel.

Press button.

"Hello. Hello," I called out. Waited. "Anyone there? Hello."

Nothing.

I waited, tried once more, and then switched channels.

Depressing the button, I called out again. "Hello? Anyone there?"

I reached for the soup bowls. My plan was to rinse them, heat water on the grill and soak all the utensils. Before taking the bowls, I called out a second time. "Hello."

Shaking my head, I put down the radio and returned to the bowls.

The hiss of static made my heart skip a beat. I spun.

"A little enthusiasm please, Faye. No one will reply to you."

My mouth dropped open. Was he checking up on me? Just to be irritating, I lifted the radio and said, "Really, Dodge?"

Smiling a little, I switched channels. After calling out a few times, I emptied the bowls, switched channels again, called out, set down the radio and filled a pot with water. I felt it was dumb, but just on the outside chance Dodge was checking up on me, I kept doing it.

Had the screen door to the deck not been open, I wouldn't have heard the hiss of static. I listened, standing in the doorway. Waiting for Dodge to say I was slacking. But the voice that came over the radio wasn't Dodge. It was male, but young.

"Hello?" he said. "Did I hear someone? Hello?"

I rushed inside and lifted the radio. "I'm here. I'm here."

Did the young man do it on purpose, or was he unaware he had the button pressed in when he screamed loudly in relief?

"Are you okay?"

"I am now. Thank God. Thank God. I thought everyone was dead."

"Are you in Kentucky?"

"Lady, I don't think my radio reaches that far. My batteries keep dying. I've been trying for days to reach someone."

The young man wasn't a child, I could tell that. "Listen to me. In case I lose you, there is a convoy leaving from Wendell Ford training

205

base in Kentucky, off of Interstate Seventy. They're headed south to Florida in eight days."

"Should I go there?"

"Yes. Yes. Go to the base. Are you close?"

"Not really. I don't know how to get there."

I exhaled hard and thought. Find out where he is, send Dodge. That was what came to mind. That and "Please let Dodge, in all his eavesdropping glory, chime in." I waited for it, for Dodge to intervene and say, "Son, where are you?" But Dodge wasn't listening. At least, I didn't think so.

"Lady?" he called out. "You there?"

"I'm here. Where are you?"

Static.

Oh, God, I thought. "Are you there?"

Nothing.

I closed my eyes tightly. All I could see was that desperate young man, falling apart because after finally making contact he'd lost it.

At least I'd got the information to him.

As I stood to finish cleaning up, I caught a glimpse of the picture of my son's basketball team that hung on the wall of my dining room.

The boy I'd talked to on the radio sounded so young. What if it had been my son? What if Mark had lived, survived the flu, and was calling out for help? I would hope some stranger, no matter how radio-ignorant she was, wouldn't give up.

So I didn't.

I put more effort and passion into trying again. I called out, and kept calling until the indicator light went from green to red and my own battery finally died. I never received an answer or heard the young man's voice again.

I prayed he was alright and that it was only the battery. He'd call again, surely he would.

A knock at the door snapped me out of it and I hurried to open it. No sooner did I unlock it than George blasted in.

"The pump worked. We got tons of gas. Gonna fill the RV and get more," he said.

Darie ran in and hugged my legs. The boys both reeked of gasoline. I ran my hand over Darie's head, absorbing the feeling of his greeting.

Dodge walked in. "Boys, wash up."

"Dodge, did you hear the radio? I made contact."

"You what?" he asked, shocked.

"A young man. But I lost it. I was able to tell him about Kentucky."

"Good. That's good. He'll radio back, I'm sure."

That's when I realized Dodge was standing by the door and not moving. "Dodge, what's wrong?"

"We have a situation."

George spoke, upbeat. "We found the teenage boy. He wasn't shot."

I gasped, though with some sort of happy shock—but immediately noticed Dodge looked confused. "Is he sick?"

"No, but he won't come in," Dodge said. "Told me he was scared. That you didn't want to see him."

"That's ridiculous. Does he know me?"

"Said he did. He told me that you called him painful."

"What the hell?" I shook my head. There was no way I knew who it was. Every person I knew was gone. There was definitely no one I would call painful. I was baffled—that wasn't me. But when I looked out the door, I realized it *was* me—just several months earlier.

When I lost my family, I shunned and pushed away anyone and anything that was a reminder of them. In my grief, I once bitterly told a teenage boy to stay away because he was like a painful memory of everything I'd lost. Now that boy stood in my driveway. Only he was no longer a hurtful reminder, but something I needed and a positive glimpse of a life I'd loved.

Standing there, scared to death, dirty and crying, was my son's best friend, Mikey.

35. REMEMBRANCE

The world had taken from me everything I loved. And it took it before the ERDS virus swept across the globe. I had nothing left but pictures and memories, and even the memories were soured with the bitterness of my tragic loss.

I was an anomaly in this quiet world. I didn't care. I woke up to death long before that pile of bodies. I woke up to loss every day; to me, the world dying was really nothing, in hindsight. We measure tragedy on how it affects us personally, and the ERDS virus didn't faze me emotionally.

I had nothing left—or so I thought.

The moment I saw Mikey, I realized I did have something. I had a tangible being that was from my own life. Not only that, but a young man I'd known since Boy Scouts. I'd watched him grow. He was a part of my son, and in some ways, I'd had a part of my son returned to me.

How fortunate I was.

But I had erred, and I had a lot of making up to do. In my selfish grief, I'd hurt that young man, and it didn't hit me until I saw him again just how much I'd hurt him.

Before, I didn't want to hear Mikey talk about Mark and their memories. Now, I did.

When Mark was killed, Mikey was around a lot. He was at the house every day, in Mark's room, trying to talk to me. Missing my son so much, I failed to see how hurt he was, because I was blinded by my own pain.

As much as me, in his own way, Mikey couldn't comprehend his loss. But unlike me, he'd reached out for a piece of Mark—me—and I'd pushed him away.

I snapped.

Three weeks after the funeral, Mikey was at the house. He was talking about how he and Mark had been in some sort of gaming tournament and how he wasn't going to do it now, and I lost it.

"Get out. Please. Leave."

I still recall the look on his face. The hurt, how lost he was.

"Mrs. Wills?"

"You look like him, act like him, and I can't look at you without my heart breaking. Every day you are here is a constant reminder of what I've lost. Leave, and never come back. You're just too painful to me."

He cried and ran out.

How horrible I'd been. How absolutely horrible, and I vowed in a single second to do everything in my power to make up for the hurt I'd caused that child. If I could.

I ran to him. He looked as if he were going to bolt—he actually backed up, but I grabbed his thin arm, yanked him close, then threw my arms around him in the biggest motherly embrace I could deliver.

He was stiff at first, and then his body almost collapsed. He grabbed on to me and buried his head in my shoulder.

Mikey was sobbing, and I cried as well.

"Mike, I am sorry, baby, I am so sorry I hurt you. I am so sorry that you were afraid to see me. I promise with everything I am, that I am here for you."

He didn't stop crying. He was a weak child, like me and Darie, left for dead and confused when he opened his eyes.

We had each other.

I was so grateful to see Mikey and hold him. Not because he was a piece of my past and of my son, but just because he was Mikey.

36. FRAME OF MIND

It wasn't long before Mikey collapsed. I didn't know what caused it—illness, weakness, hunger. He needed tending to. Dodge carried him into the house and cleaned him up for me. He then asked me to do something very hard—to find some clothes, possibly something that had belonged to Mark.

I completely froze in my tracks.

"Faye, I'm sorry, I thought maybe you had some of his clothes."

"I do."

"Can you get them? Should I put Mikey in Mark's room?"

I answered quickly. "No."

"What?"

"I haven't opened Mark or Sammy's room in months. I don't … I can't."

Reading Dodge's face was difficult. Did he understand, or was he pacifying me?

"So I should just leave him in your room?"

"Yes, and I'll look for clothes."

"Please."

I didn't go into Mark's room. I couldn't. I reached for the door knob, but I couldn't physically bring myself to enter. Instead I went to the laundry room, where I found some clothes on the shelf.

Dodge didn't say any more when he returned; he just poured a can of soup into a pot and ignited the Coleman stove that now sat on the counter. "He needs to rest, eat and comprehend," he said.

"What do you mean?"

"Where's the whiskey?"

"Wow. Cabinet above the fridge. It's not even six."

Dodge didn't reply, or respond to my comment about drinking so early. But something was up. Dodge wasn't me. He wasn't an "I need a drink" person, or at least he hadn't seemed it over the past few days.

"What's going on?" I asked.

"Something isn't right with that kid."

"Is he sick?"

"Aside from dehydration and lack of food, he's not right. It took us four times calling him for him to stop. Trust me; George yelling will wake the dead. No pun intended to the zombie fear that runs rampant around here."

"He's in shock then."

"Possibly. He didn't want to come, and that was before he knew we were with you."

"Oh, that's wrong."

"It's the truth, and I'm not saying it to be a dick." Dodge poured a drink, shot it back, then poured another. He tossed the warmed soup into a mug. "Come with me to talk to him."

I looked down. Dodge was holding out his hand to me. I didn't take it, just brushed by him and headed toward the bedroom on the first floor.

I yelled to the boys that we'd be back to make them dinner. They didn't respond; once again, Dodge had found snacks for them and they'd be on a sugar rush. His telling the boys, "No one is gonna make candy for a long time, eat up now," didn't cut it.

Mikey was lying on the bed when we walked in, eyes open. Staring almost eerily.

"Brought you soup, guy," Dodge said. "You didn't touch your water."

"I will." Mikey sat up. "I can't stay."

Dodge set down the soup. "You can't go. In fact, if you don't hydrate and eat, you won't be going anywhere much longer."

"I don't care."

I moved and sat on the side of the bed next to Mikey. "I know this is a lot to take in."

"You don't know."

"How can you say that?" I asked.

"Because you don't. You know what I'm talking about. Who did you lose?"

Dodge cleared his throat. "Okay, I know you have been through a lot—"

"Dodge," I said, stopping him. "Mikey, what can I do?"

"Let me go. Let me go find my mom."

I peered over my shoulder at Dodge, then back to Mikey. "Do you think she's still alive?"

"I don't know. I am, right? You are. He … He is. I saw my dad. I saw him die. But my mom, last I know she was only getting the fever. If I lived, how do I know she didn't? Those kids there, they're brothers. It might be a family thing."

Immediately, I thought back to what George had seen. The people waking up, only to be shot. "You're right. It might be."

"Faye," Dodge said, almost a warning.

"Have you gone home?" I asked.

"Yes. She wasn't there."

"Where have you checked?"

"Faye."

"I've been going through the bodies at the medical setup. That was where I saw her last."

I heard Dodge breathe out heavily, then he said, "That's what he was doing when I found him."

"And I'll keep looking," Mikey snapped. "Until I know. I need to know."

I placed my hand on his leg. "Mikey, I understand. I do. Was it a military setup?"

"Yes."

"Okay, then they kept track, at least at first. Did you look at any paperwork they had?"

Mikey shook his head. "Just the bodies."

"Well, then you rest tonight, eat, and we'll go tomorrow. I'll help you look. Deal?"

"You'll help me look through the bodies?"

"Every one of them if I need to." I handed him the soup. "Just eat, okay?"

Mikey nodded and took the mug. I ran my hand over his head, stood and walked to the door. Dodge followed me out.

"Faye," he whispered. "What are you doing?"

"What do you mean?"

"It's been days."

I kept walking, down the hall then to the four steps that led to the main floor. "Are you implying, Dodge, this is an impossible task?"

"Nothing is impossible, Faye. But don't you think if his mother were alive, the first place she'd look is that camp as well?"

"We're gonna look. I'm gonna help him."

"We have to get ready to leave. We have to prep the RV."

"Then you do it. I have to help Mikey."

"I watched the news, Faye. Every person that died at those local places, they didn't keep the bodies there. They put them in dump trucks."

"What's your point?"

"My point is, more than likely, she's probably at one of the big places, like my kids. You don't see me cutting into every body bag. I saw what I needed to face the truth. I have a bad feeling, a really bad feeling about that kid."

"And you don't know him. I do," I said. "I have known him since he was six years old. I have to help him."

"Okay." Dodge lifted his hands. "You help him search. I'll get things ready to leave. But you can't search forever. Eventually, instead of helping him search, you're gonna have to help him face reality."

"I will."

"I'll hold you to that," Dodge said. "Because right now, I don't know if that kid's frame of mind can handle reality."

37. LAST WOMAN

Just after we finished supper, Mikey came out of the bedroom. He spent a little bit of time with the boys, talking and playing some card game I knew Darie didn't understand.

Meanwhile, Dodge was playing with the other radio, calling out in an imitation of Hashman. Cool, calm and reserved. It was odd, because it really didn't sound like Dodge at all. I guess he was hoping to get the man in Kentucky or the boy I'd spoken to earlier. No success either way.

Mikey went back to bed, and about that point, Dodge decided he was done with the radio and was in the mood for grilled Spam. I hadn't thought anyone would ever be in the mood for grilled Spam.

With unleavened bread he'd picked up from the store, a jar of cheese whiz and Spam in hand, he fired up the grill.

George asked if he could try calling out on the radio, and Dodge simply said, "Be my guest." Who knew, dumb luck might strike again.

It was a chilly night, so we were inside; Dodge had attributed that to not being able to make clear contact. I was sitting at the dining room table, watching George, when Darie approached me with a picture of Sammy.

"Who is she?"

A lump formed in my throat. "That's my daughter."

"Did she get the flu?"

"No, she ..." How to say it, how to tell a child younger than Sammy about what had happened. "She had to go away before the flu."

"Was she my age?"

"Just about." I took the picture and stared at it. "This was her kindergarten picture."

"Did she have lots of toys?"

"I think so."

It was a conversation I didn't want to have. But how do you turn away a four-year-old boy? I gripped the picture of my beautiful daughter in my hands. She was smiling, and she still had all her baby teeth. What had happened to her hair in that picture, I'll never know. It was a mess, though I'd fixed it before school.

Just as I was at the point of asking Darie if we could not talk about her, my reprieve arrived. It came somewhere between Dodge announcing the Spam treats were done and Darie asking if he could see Sammy's room.

Hashman.

"Well, it doesn't surprise me," he said. "Another kid. Are you alone, son?"

"No, sir. Hold on."

Dodge nearly dropped his plate of unappetizing treats as he whipped the radio receiver from George's hand. "Is this Hashman in Kentucky?"

"It is. I take it you picked up my call. You're not coming through very clear, but I hear you. Speak slow. Over."

"We did," Dodge said. "We are planning on coming down. Over."

"We? As in, more than you and the child?" Hashman asked. "Over."

"Yes. Five of us."

"That's good. The move is not me. It's the military that remained on base."

"How many?" Dodge asked.

"Three soldiers. Seventy civilians. How many adults do you have?"

"Two."

Hashman let out a loud breath. "That's good to hear. Good to hear. We need adults; we have an awful lot of children down here. It's looking like it may be gender specific. We'll know more in Florida.

Supposed to be some CDC doctor down there. But we haven't located a woman yet. You?"

Dodge opened his mouth, paused and depressed the button. "Negative." He looked at me. "I'll keep an eye out though."

"Gotta make my hourly. See you soon. Where you from?"

"Pennsylvania."

"See you soon, PA. Out."

Dodge clenched the microphone in his hand and stared at the radio.

"She's a woman, ain't she?" George said. "How come you didn't tell him Faye was with us?"

"I want to keep that little tidbit to ourselves for now," Dodge said. "Just for now."

Then he did something I didn't expect. He shut down the radio. Grabbing his Spam snack and his drink, he sat at the table with me and said nothing about the exchange with Hashman. The only sound that came from Dodge's mouth was when he swept up the playing cards and stated that he hated the game Old Maid.

Something was bothering him, and it wasn't just a child's card game.

I sent the boys into the other room to settle, so I could broach the conversation with Dodge. When they were clear from the room, I fixed a drink and joined him. "That is a lot of people down there."

"Yeah, it is." Dodge flipped through the cards.

"How can I be the only woman?"

Dodge lifted his eyes. "You're not. Just …" He cleared his throat. "The only one found. There has to be others. There has to be."

"What if there aren't?"

"Then we have problems." He dropped the deck.

"Are you rethinking going down there?"

He looked at me. "It's civilization; it's a lot of people working together to rebuild, or whatever. The boys need that. Not so much rethinking going, just maybe rethinking how we're gonna go about it." He stood. "Just on the outside chance you are the last woman."

He left me hanging with a table full of scattered cards.

It scared me that they were looking for women, and I guessed it scared Dodge even more. He didn't bring it up again the rest of the evening, at least not around the boys.

Dodge set up the living room camp, got them to sleep and checked on Mikey. I was still seated at the table, this time reading by the light of the lantern, when I heard something thump to the floor. Dodge sat down across from me.

"What would you think about cutting your hair?"

"Cutting my hair? It's not that long."

"I mean buzz it."

"What?" I laughed. "Why would I …" I paused. "You want me to pretend I'm a man."

"It may not be a bad idea."

"It's a bad idea. What am I supposed to do, be a mute as well? Why are we even going then?"

"We have to go somewhere. We can't stay north. Whether we go there or somewhere else, until we know you aren't the last woman, it's the best way."

"I'll think about it." I flipped the page in the book. "What did you drop on the floor?"

Dodge lifted a backpack. I recognized it. I'd had it when I left the stadium camp. He unzipped it and emptied the contents on the table.

Stacks and stacks of drivers' licenses and identifications.

"What are you doing with those?"

"There was a reason you brought these along, and it wasn't just to remember civilization. I think it was a psychic intuition."

"For?"

"Finding people." He tossed a stack my way. "Did you look through all of these?"

"No. There are hundreds, if not a thousand."

"Good. Then start looking again." He grabbed a stack and undid the rubber band. "What was Mikey's mother's name?"

"There's no way," I said.

"Worth a shot. Didn't you say you'd help him in any way?"

My jaw dropped.

"Don't say 'really.'"

"I wasn't going to."

"Besides, what else is there to do? Again, it's worth a shot."

"You're right." I undid the rubber band. "Elizabeth Carrington. Westwood Drive."

"Elizabeth Carrington, Westwood." Dodge slowly flipped through the stack he held.

Boys asleep, Mikey resting, Dodge and I began to search through the mass of licenses. It would take a while, holding each license or identification card up to the small amount of light to read the name.

It was something to do, and it was something productive, whether it was in vain or not. In a way, I was helping Mikey. That was something I really wanted to do.

38. INSTINCT

Dodge was right. More than likely, it wasn't just some creepy thing I'd done, taking the licenses. It was a gut instinct. Maybe somewhere deep inside me I'd known I'd eventually need them.

We called it a coincidence when Dodge knew one of the women. He lifted the card, said her name then recited a laundry list of car repairs he'd done for her.

It ceased being a coincidence when he found another, and another. Either he had the most popular car repair shop in town or those bodies were from our locality. Dodge hadn't lived or worked far from my house.

The Wilkes reports still didn't make any sense to me. There were names, but none of them matched a single license we found. Colors and numbers, and dates. I recognized dates, and every so often he'd written a notation.

Either Dodge and I were talking too loudly or George couldn't sleep. In any event, he staggered into the dining room and sat at the table with us.

"What are you guys doing?"

"Searching," I said.

"For?" He reached forward and slid the clipboard to him.

"Honey, that's something I found. It won't make any sense."

"Sure it does," George said. "This is just truck numbers, locations, and the color codes are how old the bodies are. Black means they have been bagged a while."

Dodge repeated George's words almost as if he were in shock that he would say it like that. "Bagged a while?"

"Trucks came by four times a day, more at first, then less. Then not at all. That's the bodies that are still there."

I looked at the clipboard, lifted a page. "So this N-8, April 28. White? Means what?"

"It means that north region eight have a pickup of fresh bodies. If anyone was gonna wake up, it would be in that stack. We were S-12. South region 12."

"My God, you poor thing," I said. "To know this."

"It was something I did. That and collect wallets, take the licenses"—he lifted a stack of identifications—"put them in a band, and then in a box by the bodies."

"And here I thought Wilkes did this. Instead, it was an eight-year-old boy."

"In our region," he said. "I don't know who did these."

Dodge said, "You, probably. I know several of these people. They lived around there. Good job. But I am sorry you had that task."

George shrugged. I reached over and ruffled his hair.

"So if you are looking through S-12 photos, you must be looking for … for Mikey's mom."

"Wow." I huffed in disbelief. "That was pretty good. You're really smart."

Again, he shrugged. "It's a curse." He spoke nonchalantly, lifting a stack. That made me laugh.

"I was in special classes at school. Not like the special classes that Darie would have to go to. The smart kind." He looked at each picture on the licenses as he spoke, not even realizing he was making us smile. "This lady looks nice." He handed Dodge the license. "Yeah, I won Calcusolve, which was a math competition, and I was supposed to go to Harrisburg for the state spelling bee final. Guess that's not happening."

"Next thing you know, buddy," Dodge said, "you're gonna tell me you play chess."

"Doesn't everyone?"

I raised my hand. "I don't."

"Well, I do," Dodge replied. "And you're on, George. I love a good chess game, and somehow I think you'd be the one—"

He broke off and all of us jolted. Someone had knocked at the door. It startled me so much, I felt my whole body go into spasms of trembling.

Dodge jumped up, pointing to George. "Stay here. Faye, grab the baby from the living room."

Another knock. It wasn't pounding—it was gentle. "Dodge." He reached behind the waist of his pants for the revolver and pulled it out. "Dodge, seriously? You're pulling a gun?"

"You don't know."

"Yeah, I do. I'm pretty sure the bad guys aren't gonna tap on the door."

He grunted at me, stared me down for a moment, then walked to the door.

I took a step forward.

"What are you doing?" he asked

"Seeing who's there."

"Faye." He held up his hand. "Just … Just stay back."

I folded my arms. "Fine." Then I felt George move behind me; obviously he wasn't heeding Dodge's warning either.

Weapon ready, Dodge placed his foot near the bottom of the door to stop it blasting open. He turned the knob and peeked through the slight crack, then let out a deep breath and opened the door all the way.

The senior man standing outside, who looked more like a retired executive than a pandemic survivor, took off his hat and ran his fingers through his hair. "I was out looking for my daughter. I saw the light in the distance. Imagine my surprise when I got home to find most of my food was gone and my Fastball parked in your back driveway."

I let out a laugh of relief and charged forward. "Mr. Doyle."

I embraced him gratefully and welcomed him into my home. Though I made a mental note to tell Dodge about all the times he'd made fun of me for not wanting to loot my neighbors. Maybe I did have more of a psychic intuition than I'd given myself credit for.

39. LOST

Mr. Doyle didn't spend the entire night, but he did stay long enough to have a drink and tell us that he was trying to find his daughter, who was across town. He'd had no plans to return, but decided he was going to come back for his RV and then head west to find his other daughter. I can only imagine what he thought when he saw I had his RV and his car.

He was good about it. That was just Mr. Doyle. He didn't hold much hope that his daughter out west was alive, because the last they'd talked she was very sick.

He had, however, run into other survivors. "A man and a boy," Mr. Doyle said. "I was going to stay with them, but they were headed south to Kentucky and didn't want to wait for me." He didn't understand quite why.

Dodge explained what was happening, and Mr. Doyle said he'd return in the morning to start getting Fastball ready.

He didn't waste time the next morning either, coming over bright and early. I was still sleeping, my mind spinning and turning from looking at the drivers' licenses all night long. I woke to discover how good Doyle was with children. Actually, remembering how good he was. I kind of felt out of place. Dodge was being "Mr. Dad", and Doyle was a natural grandfather.

After splashing my face with a little water to freshen up, I stumbled into the kitchen just as they were talking about me shaving my head.

Doyle disagreed with Dodge. "I honestly just think they haven't found any women yet. Is it possible for a flu to be genetically specific? Who knows? I was a tax lawyer. Ask me about a Schedule C and I'll go into great detail. Ask me about germs and I'm clueless."

"It's a tough situation," Dodge replied. "If it were just her and I, then I'd really debate on joining up with a group. But the boys need that. The boys need other people, and they need someone to watch out for them."

I cleared my throat to announce my presence to the room, then poured a cup of coffee. "I'm not shaving my head, deepening my voice or pretending to be a shocked mute. Forget it."

"If you are the last woman," Dodge said, "it could be bad."

"Not yet," Doyle said. "Maybe a few months from now. Worry about it then. Right now, I think people aren't thinking that way. Or most aren't, and the few who are ... Well, you look like a big, mean guy, Dodge, no offense. But I think you wouldn't have any problem dealing with it. Rich is probably breathing a sigh of relief you found her."

"She found me."

"In jail," I added.

Doyle smiled over his coffee. "Even better."

Suddenly, I believe Doyle saw Dodge as a hardened criminal. We all shared a laugh over that, until George barreled into the room.

"He's gone," George yelled.

"Who?" I said, panicked. "Darie?"

"No, he's playing that old hand game. Mikey. He's gone. I went into the room to see if he wanted to eat or go out and he was gone."

Dodge cocked his head. "He had to have left before I got up, and that was hours ago."

"Damn it." I chugged my coffee, as hot as it was, set down the cup and headed to the kitchen. "Thank you, George."

"Whoa. Wait. Where are you going?" Dodge grabbed my arm.

"To find him."

"Let him go. He'll be back or he won't. I got a bad feeling about that kid, Faye."

"Dodge, you're wrong. He's only lost and confused, and he's gonna search every body."

"Then let him," Dodge said.

"I promised him I'd help."

"Faye, he obviously doesn't want your help."

"He doesn't know that I can end his search. You know it and I know it."

Dodge sighed, then ran his hand down his face. "Showing him his mother's license isn't going to make a difference."

"I know. But I have to try. If I can stop him from looking at one more decaying body, then that's one less nightmare that boy will face." I went into the dining room to get the license, the one I'd found in the tenth stack. The one that belonged to Mikey's mother. I retrieved it, placed it in my back pocket and went to the door.

"Faye."

"He's on foot, I know where he went. I'll find him." I opened the door, ignoring Dodge as he called out my name, and walked out.

<><><><>

When I reached the edge of my property, I remembered Rich's bike in the garage. I wasn't sure how good the tires were, but I didn't want to waste the gasoline to go only a few miles. Dodge was determinedly trying to stop me, calling my name, swearing at me. But I ignored him and stayed focused.

About a mile down the road, I heard the car pull up.

"Faye, get in," Dodge said, rolling down the window.

"You're wasting gas."

"Well, I'm here. Mr. Doyle is with the boys. Park the bike."

"I can't just leave it, it's Rich's bike."

"I'll come back for it when I do the gas run."

I kept peddling.

"Goddamn it, Faye."

I stopped. "Why do you swear at me?"

"I'm sorry, just get in. Leave the bike, I promise no one will steal it."

Reluctantly, I perched the bike against a parked car and got in the wagon with Dodge. It was a good thing I did, because when we arrived at the Walmart, Mikey was nowhere to be found.

I imagined him lost, wandering, checking every body he passed on the road. I didn't want to face the fact that we might have lost him, that he might have taken off.

Dodge headed east, telling me about another site where bodies had been taken. He and George had found it the day before, and it was where they'd come across Mikey.

We weren't even a block away and I could smell the bodies. It was rank, and I wanted to gag. I brought my shirt over my face.

How many corpses were there that the stench carried that far? We hit a military blockade before I even saw any bodies. But I heard the flies. Millions of them. Dodge was able to drive around and get close to the dump site.

Just beyond the blockade was the fence around the local high school baseball field. The field was covered in black and tan body bags, occasionally speckled with what looked like bedsheets in the high, wide mounds. As Dodge stopped the car, I saw Mikey.

He was by home plate, at the edge of the mound. He was sitting on the ground, rocking back and forth, and cradled in his arms was a body.

I glanced at Dodge. "That can't be her, can it? We found her license."

"Maybe they just took her license," Dodge suggested.

I opened the car door.

"Faye," Dodge called.

The smell was horrendous, and it hit me like a ton of bricks. My mouth instantly filled with bile. As hard as it was, I had to put that aside and focus on helping Mikey.

"Mikey!"

"Go away."

"Mikey." I stepped closer.

"I said, go away!" he shouted, his voice ragged, then looked down at the body he held. "It's over."

I was still a good twenty feet from him, but I could clearly see how rotten the body was.

"I went to homecoming with this girl," he said. "Look at her. Look at this. It's over."

"Mikey, let's go." I extended my hand.

The body rolled from Mikey's lap as he stood. "I'm not going anywhere until I find my mother."

"She's not here, Mikey."

"She is."

"No." I reached into my pocket. "When I was at the stadium, there were thousands and thousands of bodies. The military had gathered their names and identification. I took a lot of the IDs." I pulled out the license. "I'm sorry, Mikey. I am so sorry. I found your mother's license last night." I held it out to him.

Mikey surprised me in two ways then. The first was when he cried out, knocking the license from my hand and swatting me away. "You're lying!" The second surprise was that he had a gun in his hand.

I stepped back. "Where did you get that?" I asked. My body was shaking. I hated guns. I inched back even more.

"There's dead soldiers everywhere—where do you think? It wasn't hard."

Dodge must have spotted the gun, because he came racing over. Mikey swung the gun toward him.

"Put it down, Mikey," Dodge said calmly.

"No." Mikey shook his head. "This is life now? I don't want to be a part of it. My friends are dead, my family is dead. What is there left?"

"Us," I said.

Mikey laughed. It was a mad laughter. "Oh my God, are you serious? Are you fucking serious? You think you're a reason for me to want to live? You didn't want to live. I didn't understand it then—I do now. You know, I hated you for pushing me away. Hated you."

"I'm sorry."

"No, I'm sorry. I'm sorry I called the police when you took those pills. I'm sorry I kept checking on you, scared to death that you were gonna kill yourself. I kept thinking, Mark wants me to watch his mom. But you didn't. I shouldn't have stopped you. I was wrong for not letting you die."

"No, you weren't. You weren't wrong. Please, Mikey, just put down the gun."

"And do what? Go to Kentucky? Make new friends, call you 'Mom' and Dodge here 'Dad'? Right. People aren't replaced, and you know it. There's nothing to live for. I don't want to live in this world, Mrs. Wills."

"I want you to." Speaking gently, I slowly reached out to him. "Come with me, Mikey. We'll talk, work this out. I really want you to live."

"No, you don't," he said coldly. "And I don't think you really want to live either. Your kids are dead, your husband is dead. Yeah …" He nodded. "You don't. Here's what I took from you." He extended the gun.

It all happened so fast. I saw the gun, I felt the fear, and then Dodge's body slammed into mine just as the gun went off. We careened hard to the ground and landed with a thud. Dodge was heavy on top of me—I could barely move.

My mind spun. I was trying to understand. Mikey had shot at me. I felt a pain in my left arm, and I wasn't sure if I was having a heart attack or if I'd been hit.

Dodge lifted some of his weight, and I turned my head, catching my breath. Then I saw Mikey.

The gun was to his head.

He looked right at me, as if he'd been waiting for me to see him.

"No!" I screamed loud and long.

Bang.

40. TOO FAR GONE

It was the second most traumatic event in my life. Not even waking up among a pile of decomposing bodies measured up to identifying my family at the morgue or seeing a sixteen-year-old boy kill himself.

Mikey had taken his own life and made eye contact with me as he did it. It seemed to happen in slow motion. The way he looked at me, that eerily peaceful expression, then watching the spray of blood.

It was too much.

Far too much.

I screamed. In relentless agony, I cried out, trying to make my way to Mikey's lifeless body.

Dodge held me back.

I had actually been shot. His aim had been dead on. I was a moment away from that end result I'd sought just a few months earlier. Had it not been for Dodge's quick interference, I would have been dead.

Not that it mattered.

I'd flung my arm out just as Dodge tackled me from the left. In that split second as his body hit mine, the bullet grazed across my lower bicep. If he'd been a fraction of a second later, the bullet would have hit my chest.

Dodge stopped holding me back; I suppose he didn't want to add to my injury. I broke free and raced to Mikey's body. As if I expected him to still be alive. I shouldn't have done it.

I stopped a little way away; seeing what was left of him up close would have been too much to handle. But despite his obvious wounds, I noticed something else.

There was a look of peace on Mikey's face.

He'd opted out of this life. Life … If that's what you could call it.

I must have been bleeding badly, because through my shock, I was aware of Dodge wrapping his shirt around my arm. I went through stages. Screaming, crying, hysteria—then quiet.

I stared out the car window all the way back. Dodge's voice sounded like it was in a can.

"We'll get you home. Figure out a way to close that up. It's a flesh wound."

I didn't respond. The only thing I said was "Rich's bike," when I saw we'd passed it.

There was no pain; it had subsided, and I figured that was my body shutting down in shock. The reality of how badly I was bleeding hit me when Dodge carried me back into the house and I heard all the reactions.

"Good God, what happened?" Mr. Doyle asked.

"She was shot."

"The kid?"

"Yeah."

"Where's Mikey?" asked George. "Is he okay?'

"No," replied Dodge, carrying me into the den.

Darie screamed and cried; I heard Mr. Doyle trying to calm him down. I was in such a state that nothing was really registering the way that it should.

Dodge placed me on the couch. "You'll be okay. It was bleeding pretty bad."

"I don't care."

"Well, I do. I'll see if Mr. Doyle has any experience in this. If not, you're stuck with me fixing it. I can do it, but it won't be pretty."

"I don't care. Mikey's dead."

"Mikey took his own life. I am sorry you had to see that. I'm sorry he decided this world wasn't for him. But he almost took you with him, and that is what I'm thinking about. I'll be right back." He leaned over me, staring. He gently ran his hand over my face, then left.

I lifted my uninjured arm to my eyes, and began to cry.

Mikey had taken his own life, and I'd been a catalyst. He couldn't process the loss of my son, and I'd compounded that by pushing him away rather than helping him. He was already fragile when the world fell ill. A fragility I could have stopped.

Mikey had been the last living part of my previous life. I'd watched him die, and I somehow kept thinking it was a sign.

I blamed myself. I was sinking to a new low, and I couldn't help but feel it was all my fault that Mikey was dead. My fault that he'd killed himself. It was something I would have to live with for the rest of my life.

Or would I?

41. DECISIONS

The day after Mikey died was a blur. I self-medicated with large amounts of alcohol and sleeping pills—a deadly combination, but I didn't really care.

The day he died, it hurt. It hurt so badly and was such a reminder that I just didn't want to deal with it, so the next day I closed off. The third day I didn't take the sleeping pills, but I drank, enough to feel numb. Enough to be like I used to be, after the accident.

I shut down.

It was almost as if Mikey's death was some sort of wake-up call, screaming at me that I wasn't meant to survive, that any life I had on earth was meant to be filled with pain and disappointment.

A couple times both Darie and George came in to see me, asking if I was going to pack. They talked enthusiastically about how Dodge had found tons of gas for the RV, and how Mr. Doyle was showing them how to use the CB radio that was already in Fastball.

My depressed state increased my suspicions about this Kentucky move. Even if it was a military base, how did we know it was the military there now? How did we know it was anything good? They could be sadists waiting to prey on the hopeless and helpless.

I expressed my feelings, and even Dodge said he understood where I was coming from.

Until May sixteenth. Three days after Mikey's death, three days in which I was shut down in that room, an affirmation of the Kentucky camp arrived. Apparently, Mr. Doyle had made an impression on the man and the boy who were traveling south.

"Faye, come quick." Dodge poked his head into the room. "Bud is talking to that man he met. He's radioing."

He disappeared before I'd even put my feet on the floor. It took me a moment to realize "Bud" was Mr. Doyle.

I heard the radio as I left my room. It seemed the man and the boy had made it to Kentucky, to the training center, and found Hashman.

"It's a good thing, Bud, it really is," the man was saying. "I had to tell you because I know you were leery about coming down. They need you. They do. I feel good. Hopeful. Finally. You have to see, Bud, it's all kids. All but a handful. Kids. Life will go on."

"That's an awesome thing, Jim. I'm glad you radioed," Mr. Doyle said. "I really am, because I was worried."

"No need. Tell me you're still coming."

"We are."

Jim began spouting routes. He said he'd had to take a longer way because so many roads were jammed with traffic or closed. He and the boy had taken nearly five days to get there. Now he was explaining the best route for Mr. Doyle.

Mid-directions, I left the dining room. I didn't need to hear that they had to go east and take that road and this one. On my way back to my bedroom, I thought about the young man I'd spoken with on the radio. I'd never made contact with him again. I wondered if he'd made it to Kentucky. Maybe he was just listening and couldn't call out.

Back in my room, I sat on the edge of the bed and poured another glass of bourbon.

There was a single knock on the door and Dodge walked in. "Hey."

"Hey." I looked up.

"Pretty encouraging about Kentucky, huh?'

"Yes, it is."

"Got to tell you, Faye, I was worried like you that it was a bad thing. But that guy's voice, he was excited. And how about there being all kids down there?"

"Yes, I heard." I took a huge gulp of my drink. "How about that?"

"How's the arm?"

"Fine."

"Have you started packing your things yet? I see you still have pictures out." Dodge walked to the nightstand and lifted up a photo of my kids. I grabbed it from him and set it down.

"I guess the pictures are the last thing you'll bring. Are you ... Are you gonna take anything from the kids' rooms? I know you said—"

I cut him off. "I haven't been in there."

"I see." He walked over to the door and closed it.

The look on his face made me feel like I was back in school, waiting on the principal because I was in trouble.

"Faye, I don't know what to do here. I don't."

"What do you mean?"

"Tell me what to do. I thought, you know, we were becoming friends. I thought we were planning. But ... I know you've been through a rough time."

I barked a laugh and took a drink.

"We all suffered about Mikey."

"No." I set down the glass. "You knew it was coming. You knew he was unstable. How many times did you say something to that effect? You saw a teenage boy kill himself. I saw ... the last part of my world drop to a pile of bodies. I saw that part of my life explode, and I caused it. I made that happen."

"No, you didn't."

"Yeah, I did. It started after Mark's death."

"He said you took pills."

"Yep. I did. I should have died."

"Who caused that?"

"I'm sorry?"

"Who made you take the pills? Who caused you to want to die?"

"No one. It was my choice."

"Exactly," Dodge said. "Just like it was Mikey's. I don't expect you to heal from this right away. I don't. This was a personal loss to you. But we need you."

I shook my head and started to refill my glass.

"And we don't"—Dodge snatched the bottle from my hand—"need you to be a drunk."

"That's who I am."

"No, it isn't. Faye, you're shutting us out. Don't."

"I have to. I have to shut you out, and I've been doing that on purpose."

"Why?"

"Because I'm not going."

"What?" He sounded breathless.

"I'm not going to Kentucky. I'm not. That's why I am withdrawing, that's why I haven't packed. I'm not going."

"Why?"

"It's not for me, Dodge. And there's a laundry list."

"Then spill it." Dodge sat on the bed next to me. "If there's a laundry list of reasons, let me hear them."

I stared down at my hands as I spoke, not wanting to look at Dodge, to see his expression—or lack of one. "This house, this is where I belong. The memories I have here can't fit in a box."

"That's bullshit. Memories are in your mind, and that goes everywhere."

"It's more than the mind—it's the smells, sights. The kids are another reason. I can't take the worry. I can't take or chance facing something happening to another child I'm close to. I'd rather not know them, or care for them, than be hurt again. And another reason—you. If I am the last woman on earth, then how fair is that to you? You'll spend more time worrying about protecting me. It will be on your mind constantly."

"We don't know that. We can work that out."

"No, we can't, and we don't know—you're right. But I do know you asked me to shave my head."

"That's not a reason not to go," Dodge said.

"Yeah, it is, because that told me you were worried about me."

"Yeah, let's be realistic, Faye. If you are the last woman, that's a scary prospect. It is. Do you think it will be any better up here alone?"

"I do. It's better for me to be alone."

Dodge chuckled, but it sounded forced. He stood. "What are you going to do? Wave goodbye and then stay here and die?"

I looked up.

Dodge laughed again, then turned away. "Unbelievable. After what we've been through."

"Been through? Dodge, I've known you two weeks. We've been though nothing. I drank myself into oblivion to escape a dead world—and I woke up to a dead world. Mikey was the last thing remaining of everything I loved, and I watched him die. Almost as if on purpose, as if he was reserved for me to see."

"That's bullshit." Dodge spun to me. "You can care about people. You can care about the kids. George. Darie …"

"I don't want to! Caring means chancing hurt. I've had enough."

"We've all had enough. We just have to move on. Survive."

I shook my head. "There is more to being alive than just surviving. There's the will and the need to be alive, to feel alive. For that, it takes life. Sadly, me staying here, me dying, is just a formality. My life ended months ago. I'm now just catching up to where I need to be."

Dodge shook his finger, tried to speak, then with a wave of his arm, walked to the door. "You're wrong. You are wrong. You'll realize it. Then it will be too late."

"It's my loss then."

"No, it's not. It's a loss to everyone that deserved a chance to know you. But it's your choice, and I won't ask you to change your mind."

He walked out, slamming the door behind him.

I just sat there and finished my drink.

42. GOODBYE

"I'm not going to try to change your mind," Mr. Doyle said. "I don't want you to think that's why I wanted to steal a moment."

"I know." I nodded. It was just after daybreak; Dodge had decided to wait an extra day. He probably thought that if he stuck around I'd change my mind, or maybe he was hoping to miss the convoy.

"Your choice is your choice," Mr. Doyle said. "When Rich and the kids were killed, I remember saying to Becca that my God, were you brave. You must be the bravest person I've met. It takes a lot to love in this world, and to keep going when it's gone. I don't know how I'm doing it now. We all make choices. There are no wrong ones now."

"Thank you." I embraced him. "Watch the kids."

"I will. They're a heck of a focus."

The kids.

It hadn't been my choice not to tell them I wasn't going. Dodge wanted to spare them being hurt or thinking it was something they'd done. He also knew they'd not quite understand why I'd opted to stay behind. So he'd told them I would join them later, after they found more women, because I didn't want to be the only girl.

George gave me a huge hug and a kiss on the cheek. He was excited about leaving, and said to me, "I hope when we get there, there will be girls. Will it work if there are little girls?"

"Yes, it will." I hugged him.

"Good. Listen to the radio, because we're gonna call."

"You behave and take care of your brother. You're all he's got."

George looked at me quizzically. "No, I'm not anymore. He has Mr. Doyle, Dodge and you. There's a lot more people today than I thought we had last week."

He kissed me, and then Darie came over. He was holding something up, a truck he'd tried to build out of Lego.

"For me?" I asked.

"For you. I made it."

"Oh, honey, why don't you take it? It's so nice."

"It's for you." He smiled. "A flying truck. You have something to play with when we're gone."

I clutched the truck. Its wheels were wobbly, and it had a propeller on top; when I grasped it, the propeller fell off.

"That's okay." Darie picked it up. "It fixes. Look how easy it goes back together."

I never was any good with Lego, and when I reattached the propeller, I put it in the wrong place.

Darie reached up to readjust it, but stopped. "That looks good. Don't worry if you break it again. Just fix it. It can look different and it's still the same. It's still a toy." He said it with such innocence, and a smile as wide as his face.

"I'll try to keep it as it is."

"Okay." He gave me a quick hug. A pretty good one for a four-year-old. I kissed him and hugged him back.

He darted out the door with his brother, waving.

Dodge.

He was all that remained, and it was his turn to say goodbye.

"I told you I won't ask you to change your mind," he said. "I've been good about that."

"Yes, you have."

"Just know, I want you to."

I lowered my head. I thought he was going to leave—he turned as if he were about to, then stopped. "Faye." He sighed. "I have never begged anyone for anything in my entire life." He stepped closer to me. "Please. Please. Change your mind and go with us."

"Dodge …"

"It's not too late. It isn't."

"Please don't do this. Just … Just say goodbye."

"There's gas on top of the wagon."

"I know. You shouldn't have done that."

Dodge shook his head. "I had to. It's for you. There's a map on the front seat and a radio. Channel seven. I'll have the CB on seven. Radio me. It's all ready for you if you change your mind."

"I won't. You better go."

He stepped in to me and put his arms tightly around me, pressing his cheek to mine. I could feel his breath against my ear, and then he spoke in a heavy whisper. "I know you said you have nothing to live for. But you do. You just have to see it and want it. I pray to God you do." He put his lips to my cheek, held them there a moment, then pulled back.

"Be careful. Goodbye, Dodge."

He shook his head and laid his hand on my cheek. "Not goodbye. I refuse to believe that. Refuse." Another kiss to my forehead and he moved back. "Thank you for saving my life that day. I wish I could have saved yours."

I wanted to say, "You did, you stopped that bullet," but that wasn't what he meant.

Without any further hesitation, Dodge walked outside. Standing in the doorway, I watched him get into Fastball. He didn't look back.

Mr. Doyle waved from the front seat. Dodge never looked at me. He pulled out of the driveway and drove down the street.

I stayed until they were no longer in sight.

Dodge, Mr. Doyle, George and Darie … had left.

43. REVELATION

A silence consumed the house, and it was unlike any I had ever experienced. It didn't happen right away; hours later, just as evening set in, so came the odd silence.

I remember, before Rich and the kids were killed, how I'd savored the silence of the house when they'd go to the store. I'd lie on the couch, close my eyes, and always, no matter what time it was, take a nap.

It was a peaceful silence.

When they died, I hated the quiet. It had become hurtful. I replaced it with a television that was always on in the background. I'd fall asleep to its noise.

But no matter the circumstances, it was never truly silent. There were birds, cars, planes and people making noise outside.

Now was the first time that not only was I completely alone in my home, but I was enveloped by a new silence—a scary one.

A part of me waited for Dodge or the boys to radio. After all, George had said he would. But the message never came. I felt a shiver of a fear that they'd got into an accident. Then I tapped deep in my gut and knew they just weren't going to contact me. Dodge had made the separation.

I drank a lot after they left, staring at the half bottle of sleeping pills I intended to take the next day. I wasn't ready for them yet. I still had a couple things to do.

The deck was my nightly routine, but now it was different. The whole house had taken a different feel, and I couldn't put my finger on what it was. After my family died, it had been a lonely house. For some reason, it felt even lonelier, and I couldn't figure out why.

Perhaps it was the alcohol.

With the throw blanket from the couch draped over me, I fell asleep on the deck.

<><><><>

I woke the next morning to the sun beating down, an unusually hot day, and a horrendous stench. The smell from the bodies left out for trash was permeating the air. They'd been out for a while, but for some reason, this morning it was as if I stood in the middle of a pile of them.

The candle had burned to the holder, and I grabbed the blanket and went inside. I shut the windows; I hated the thought of it, but I knew I had to.

I grabbed a bottle of water from the counter and reached for the tin coffee percolator that Dodge had grabbed at the home store.

But my hand hit air.

He took the coffee pot? I dismissed my irritation at a lack of caffeine and being slightly hung over. I still had instant from the local coffee shop, and I put water on the Coleman stove to heat.

While it boiled, I downed some more water, and noticed Dodge had taken all but two packs. In fact, he'd taken a lot of the supplies he'd gathered. Nothing I'd had prior to his arrival, but he'd taken what he'd looted from the neighbors and stores. There was a box of supplies on the counter, maybe three days' worth.

No sooner did I think about going to find more than I realized I wouldn't need to. Dodge had taken it all because, in his mind, it was probably a waste to leave them.

Soon enough I'd be a corpse in a bed, rotting through to the mattress, only to be found sometime later by looters—or maybe not at all.

Water boiled, coffee ready, I took a moment to enjoy it and allow it to work its way into my bloodstream. I always thought more clearly after coffee. I pulled up a stool and stared out the kitchen window while I sipped.

The sun was so bright. What day was it? May nineteenth, a Friday. In my previous life I'd be at work, waiting to take a break, because

I just didn't have the patience to wait until lunch. I only worked while the kids were in school.

My kids.

I closed my eyes, took a deep breath and finished my coffee.

Today is as good a day to die as any, I thought. I'd heard that somewhere, I didn't know where. Some television show. But it was. It was a good day to die.

At that point any day was.

I believed I was ready. Ready to take that final step, ready to meet my maker, if there was one. Face Him with my decision and hoped there'd be mercy. Surely there'd be forgiveness.

Surely I'd see my family again. After all, that was why I'd chosen to leave the world. There wasn't enough for me to hold on to life; too much lay on the other side.

I stood and looked out the window. What a beautiful, glorious day. It was almost cruel, God showing beauty among all the death that was scattered about.

Despite the green of life, the sun, all that I saw, all I felt was death.

Or so I thought.

I set down my cup. There were a few things I wanted to do before taking those pills. A few things I had to resolve.

I'd always loved the layout of my house. My kitchen led into a nice foyer that actually showed my open living room. The house was split-level, and as I walked across the foyer to the stairs, I passed the table in the hall. Immediately, I saw the little truck Darie had built for me.

It made me smile, and I picked it up. The propeller fell off.

"Damn it." I bent down and picked it up. I really never was any good with Lego; Mark used to get so frustrated with me when I—

That thought made me pause.

Mark. My son had loved Lego as soon as he figured out what it was. Taking a breath, holding on to the toy, I walked up the short flight of stairs to the next level.

I hadn't noticed it the day before, but I did now as I passed the den. The pictures, the family photos that had been spread across Rich's desk and on the walls … weren't there.

No. I stepped into the den. The walls looked bare; I lost my ability to breathe, and then immediately filled with anger when I saw the box on the desk.

Someone, probably Dodge, had packed those pictures.

How dare he? How dare he touch pictures of my family? I reached into the box. The first one I pulled out was a family photo, one of those cheesy ones I'd thought were awesome at the time, but really it was just a studio portrait, an attempt to make us look good. I laughed. We'd all worn white shirts, and Mark got a pizza stain on his. I'd wanted to kill him. I'd wanted that picture to be perfect.

It wasn't, but neither were we as a family. No family was.

Calming down, I told myself Dodge had only removed them to help me, and they were only pictures.

I'd return for the box. The toy still in my grip, I started to leave, but stopped again. I first peered slowly over my shoulder, then spun around.

Rich's books were gone. Not all of them, but the old fiction books he'd collected, the classic paperbacks. There wasn't a box. Apparently Dodge had taken them, too.

Okay, now I was mad. I wished for a moment that he'd radio so I could yell at him. No … no. I calmed down. What did I need books for?

Onward.

I went up the next set of stairs to the level of the house I hadn't been to since the kids had been killed. I froze on the top step. My head was spinning, and I felt a little faint. It was like I was walking in a dreamlike state. Even when Mikey used to go to Mark's room, I never went up. I'd just holler for him to come down.

But it was time. I wanted, and needed, to go into my children's rooms.

Sammy's room was first. After a brief hesitation, I turned the knob and opened the door. When I stepped into the room I was hit by a wave of emotions, and I couldn't help groaning. The room was exactly as she'd left it three and a half months earlier.

The blinds were messed up from where she'd peeked out, and her bed was as badly made as any five-year-old's. There were shoes everywhere, six or seven changes of clothes on her chair. She must have flipped through her wardrobe choices before leaving that day. Her dollhouse was on the floor, figures still in position.

"Oh, baby." My eyes were heavy, welling with tears as I reached down for one of the dolls. "I miss you so much."

Inhaling deeply, I took in the scent of her room. Maybe it was my imagination, or maybe it had just been sealed in there. I grabbed the pillow from her bed and walked out of the room, leaving the door open.

Mark's room. I knew it would be touched, different, because Mikey had been up there a lot after Mark died.

Mark's room was like a display of who he'd been, full of contrasts. One side showed the teenager, the other the boy. There were video game controllers on the bed, clothes scattered, soda cans everywhere.

It was when I turned around, Sammy's pillow in my arm, Darie's truck in the other hand, that I saw it. The Lego shelf.

There were shelves all around Mark's room— trophy shelf, picture shelf, bookshelf—but this one held his lifetime collection of Lego models, which he'd been making since he was four years old.

The same age as Darie.

They went from good to amazing. He'd kept the ones he was most proud of.

In the middle of the shelf there was a vehicle with a propeller. I heard Mark's young voice.

"Mom, don't touch it. You'll break it."

"I can fix it."

"You won't fix it right. It won't look the same."

"It's still a truck, right?"

My eyes shifted down to Darie's toy, and I heard him speak then.

"That looks good. Don't worry if you break it again. Just fix it. It can look different and it's still the same."

Still the same.

Different package. The idea was the same.

"Maybe you need a focus," Dodge said, "How about a kid?"

I remember that when he said that, for a moment I was angry. It's not like a new dog—a new kid wasn't going to replace my own. But that wasn't what he meant. A need, a focus.

"I lost my life months ago. I have nothing left."

I flashed back to my last conversation with George.

"You behave and take care of your brother. You're all he's got."

"No, I'm not anymore. He has Mr. Doyle, Dodge and you. There's a lot more people today than I thought we had last week."

"You're all he's got."

"No, I'm not."

Stop.

I was getting emotional, and it wasn't over my children. It was time; it was time to end my debate, my suffering, my need to die.

Turning again to leave Mark's room, I was faced with an empty shelf. What had been on it? I struggled to think.

The games. All of Mark's board games.

Gone? Dodge had taken them, too?

I was furious. He'd probably taken them for the kids, but still. It was my house, my stuff. He'd looted my home as if it were any other house that belonged to a dead person.

I screamed out his name, venting my frustration and anger.

And in that moment, I wondered what was wrong with me.

One moment sad, the next laughing—angry, happy, furious. Why was I such a seesaw of emotions? Why? Because I was alive.

Dodge had stolen from me, taken my belongings from my home as if I were already dead. He'd had every right to; I'd proclaimed to him that I was dead.

Truth is, I wasn't.

"You are wrong. You'll realize it. Then it will be too late." Dodge's voice reverberated in my head.

"No, Dodge, you're wrong. It's not too late." I rushed from Mark's room.

At least, I hoped it wasn't.

44. LIVING

The revelation had come, and I was grateful. Whether it was too late or not, it didn't matter. I needed that revelation. I'd been so focused on dying, I hadn't seen that I was still alive.

Afraid to care or feel because I was scared of losing someone only meant I wasn't as dead inside as I'd thought. And I'd rather care about someone than not feel at all. Caring was a focus. Being needed was a focus. And not only was I going to care for George and Darie, I would be needed by them.

Sammy and Mark were the loves of my life. They would never be replaced, but they weren't really gone. They were with me, with every breath I took, every memory I had; in my heart and soul they were with me.

Like Dodge had said, memories were mobile. I had to be too.

My hardheadedness had caused me to miss my chance to leave, but perhaps I'd really needed to come to the decision on my own. Alone, in my house, facing it all.

My missing items. Dodge hadn't done it to be spiteful or criminal; he'd done it because over the course of just two weeks, he'd learned who I was. He knew that taking my things would spark enough anger in me that I'd realize I wasn't dead inside, or I'd find him just to yell at him.

In either case, once again, Dodge was right.

He was so certain I would change my mind, so cool and callous about it. I half expected to find him waiting on the road.

He had my car ready, gas cans stacked on top, a map marked with a route and a radio. Hell, he'd even had the food and water ready to go. I'd seen it, but it didn't register until I had my revelation.

There were still things I wanted to take. Photos, toys, clothes. I packed them. My house wasn't going to be destroyed, and I fixed it in my mind that one day I'd return.

Prior to the accident, and even after, I was scared of everything. Before Rich and the kids died, I was scared of movies, scared to walk to the park, scared to drive at night. After they left me, I was scared to laugh, to feel, to live.

For some strange reason, when I should have been scared of the prospect of making the long drive to Kentucky, I wasn't.

Maybe it had a little to do with being the last woman.

I raided my son's room for clothes. A baggy baseball shirt, those damn old cargo pants I used to hide and a cap. They would hide my gender—as long as I didn't speak.

It was already after noon when I finally had everything ready to go. The convoy was leaving the next day. Dodge really had done everything to make the car ready, including a sleeping bag and flashlights.

The map was marked with notes. Dodge had written on a Post-it that I had to go east, then south, then west. What should have been a simple, six-hundred-mile trip had turned into nearly nine hundred miles. To get there before the convoy, I'd have to leave right away and only stop for gas and bathroom breaks.

I could do it. I really could.

As a matter of fact, I only looked back at my house once as I left. Sitting on the front seat were Sammy's doll, Mark's baseball trophy and Darie's truck.

I tried to radio Dodge on channel seven, then realized I was probably well out of range.

Mixed emotions and thoughts raced through my mind. What if Dodge had been ambushed, what if that man who'd radioed had lied and was holding them at gunpoint? What if ...?

The worst part of the trip was struggling with the gas cans when I had to pull over to refuel. I never saw another person or car. Then again, I wasn't looking. I was focused on getting to my destination. What I didn't take into account was the fact that the roads would get so dark, I couldn't travel at night. It was just impossible, especially on the country routes. The dark, winding roads became increasingly dangerous, and against my wishes I pulled over. I'd leave again as soon as the sky lightened.

It was scary. My imagination worked over time; I was frightened of things that weren't real. Bigfoot, walking dead, ax murderers. Maybe the latter was a possibility, but considering I hadn't seen a soul, I doubted some ax-wielding madman in a mask was going to come out of the trees.

It was during the night, surrounded by the dark woods, that I started to doubt myself. Was I really meant to find Dodge and the kids? Was it fair to him to have to take me under his wing, especially if I was the last female standing? Maybe my fate was to stay back at my house, live out my lonely last days until I got up enough courage to take those pills.

Then it hit me—fate. I decided that night to leave it to fate.

Since I'd woken up on that pile of bodies, everything had been a series of signs and instincts.

Fate.

Taking those identification cards led me to the truth about Mikey's mom. The suitcase and the squeaky wheel led me to Dodge.

Dodge got me home. His insistence found the boys—and so on and so on.

It was all fate stepping in, and I would place everything in its hands.

If the convoy was gone when I got there, I'd take it as a sign that I hadn't been meant to go.

I was prepared for that.

I was prepared to see Dodge and that glorious RV as well.

That was my mindset as I left the next morning at first light, and I turned off the radio. I was going to make it. The convoy would still be there. I was absolutely sure of it.

The clock had barely hit seven when I crossed into Kentucky, and I started to doubt it all when I got lost searching for the back roads that would lead me to Interstate 70. The route was marked as cleared, but I ran into a roadblock and had to use the map to find another way.

I made it to the interstate just before it passed through Central City. There was no movement, no people. Then, as I was getting closer to the Ford training facility, I slowed down.

There was a huge banner made from a bedsheet hanging on the side of a ranch-style home to my right. It read "Hashman."

For a moment I couldn't drive on. I paused, full of emotion. Something about that sign told me I'd been wrong to be so pessimistic about the Kentucky man's motives. It was a simple house, with a swing set and a doghouse.

Signs of Hashman's life.

Life.

I began to drive again, not fast, because I didn't want to hit one of the many kids that were supposedly at the training area. The sign for it appeared just outside Central City, and then I saw the entrance not far ahead.

I was there. I'd made it.

Filled with excitement, I drove up to the gate, expecting to reach a barrier or someone standing guard.

There was no one there. The base was open.

Still, it was huge. They had to be there, maybe further back inside.

However, once I'd pulled inside and spent some time driving around, I knew.

I was too late.

They were gone.

In some last, ridiculous state of hope, one I hadn't had since before the accident, I drove around the main area, then finally stopped the car.

No.

I threw it in park. I got out of the car and did a Dodge, beeping the horn and shouting, "Hello!"

I did it again, then again.

What was I doing?

I'd failed. My soul was crushed. I felt like my chest had caved in; I couldn't breathe. Overcome with the emotions that raged inside me, I dropped to my knees and started to sob.

I was wrong. I'd asked fate to give me an answer, and it did. I wasn't meant to move on, I wasn't meant to live. I'd wanted so badly to find a sign, and I'd been handed an empty base.

It was over.

My single chance to move on, to gain something back, was gone.

Or was it?

As I lowered my head, contemplating my next move, searching deep within myself and my tears for an answer, I got one. A young voice called out from behind me.

"You missed the convoy too, huh?"

I raised my head.

"I thought, you know, I'd make it, but I ran into some road-blocks."

That voice. That voice. I knew that voice.

I stood, spinning around.

He was about twenty, maybe younger, and he stood not far from me. His hair was a little long, and he was thin.

"Did you …" I stepped closer to him. "Did you talk to a woman on the radio, and she told you about this place?"

He breathed out so hard, he wheezed. "Oh my God." He rushed over to me. "Was that you?"

"That was me." I grabbed his hands.

"Thank you. Thank you."

"What happened to you?"

"I dropped the radio, and I tried—I tried to find you guys again, but when I couldn't, I just headed here."

"Oh, I am so glad to see you." I placed my hand on his face.

"But everyone's gone. What are we gonna do?"

"I didn't know at first, but I do now. We're gonna find them." I grabbed his hand and tugged him to the car. "Get your stuff."

"Can we?"

"We'll try. I was hoping fate would give me a sign. Then you called out."

"I was hoping the same thing." The young man snatched up a duffel bag and tossed it in the car.

I got in, waited for him. He looked at the toys on the seat.

"Put them in the back, gently," I said, seeing his confusion.

He did, then slid in and nodded at the radio. "You gonna try to call?"

"I am." I started the car. "See, long story—I can tell it as we go. But my party left before me. I was going to stay back, and then I changed my mind."

"Maybe, you know, you were supposed to arrive late to find me."

He looked so innocent, and so young. "Maybe," I said. "Faye." I held out my hand. "Faye Wills."

He shook my hand. "Nice to meet you, Faye. I'm Tyler. Tyler Cash."

Shocked, I pulled my hand away. "As in Dodge? Dodge Cash?"

His eyes widened. "You knew my dad?"

A cascade of chills shot up my arms and back. My eyes welled up. I really had been meant to stay behind; there was another reason, far and beyond me having to realize I had to live. I had to give Dodge that reason as well. "Knew? No. I *know* your dad."

"He's alive?" Tyler's voice was rough with emotion.

I just smiled, looked at the radio. It was on channel seven. I said a short prayer in my head. *Please let them be in radio range.* Then, with every ounce of hope I could muster, I grabbed Tyler's hand and turned on the radio.

"This is Faye. Faye calling. This is Faye, looking for Fastball. Over."

Nothing.

"Try again," Tyler urged. "Please try again."

"This is Faye. Channel seven. Looking for Fastball. Over."

Nothing. Static.

"Oh my God—Faye." It was Dodge.

Tyler was breathing heavily. "My dad."

I nodded. "Dodge, I'm on the base. Where are you guys?"

"About thirty miles away. We just left there. Faye, I'll pull over. I'm pulling over. Get on 181 South, it's clear. You can't miss me. I'm waiting. We're waiting." The words were coming fast. "And Faye, wait until you see. Wait until you see how many kids there are. It's amazing."

"I'm on my way. And Dodge ..."

"Yeah."

I looked at Tyler. "I have a surprise for you."

"You're a surprise, Faye."

"No," I said, "this is better. See you soon. Over."

"Out."

I put down the radio and, with a glance at Tyler, turned the car around.

Dodge hadn't said if there were any women or girls, but I guess it didn't matter. At that moment in time, I was filled with hope.

Hope and reason.

I'd been dying inside before the world ended, and it had taken a dead world to show me I had to live. To give me a reason to live. It was ironic, and yet wonderful.

I was indeed moving on. Finding life again. Like that toy truck, I was piecing it together. It wasn't going to look the same, but in the end, it was still life. I had to embrace it.

I would.

THE LAST WOMAN 2

With no desire to live in a world void of all human life, Faye sets a goal of making it home to die. Then she encounters Dodge and two young boys, who ignite a spark long lost in her: the will to live.

Following radio calls, they discover they are not alone and decide to join a growing camp of survivors. But another discovery threatens their new-found safety and the rules begin to change. As they desperately try to find a safe haven and figure out their place in this new world, Faye must weigh the decision of what she *wants* to do against what she *should* do.

The continuation of man's existence seems to rest with Faye.

ABOUT THE AUTHOR

Jacqueline Druga is a native of Pittsburgh, PA. Her works include genres of all types but she favours post-apocalypse and apocalypse writing.

For updates on new releases you can find the author on:

Facebook: @jacquelinedruga

Twitter: @gojake

www.jacquelinedruga.com